THE NIGHT BEFORE DEAD

Also by Kelly Meding

The Dreg City Series
Three Days to Dead
As Lie The Dead
Another Kind of Dead
Wrong Side of Dead
Requiem For The Dead
The Night Before Dead

The MetaWars Series
Trance
Changeling
Tempest
Chimera

Writing As Kelly Meade

The Cornerstone Run Series
Black Rook
Gray Bishop
White Knight

THE NIGHT BEFORE DEAD

KELLY MEDING

The Night Before Dead
Copyright © 2016 by Kelly Meding

All rights reserved. This book or any portion thereof may not be reproduced or used in any manner whatsoever without the express written permission of the publisher except for the use of brief quotations in a book review.

Printed in the United States of America
First Edition, 2016
ISBN: 978-0-9899188-3-1
www.kellymeding.com

Cover Art by Robin Ludwig Design, Inc.
Interior Design by Penoaks Publishing, http://penoaks.com

PROLOGUE

If you'd have told me a week ago that I would be sitting across a conference table from an elf, about to listen to what he had to say, I'd have told you to go to hell. Might have even punched you in the mouth for good measure. Elves had been nothing except trouble in the brief period of time that they'd been a part of my life.

An elf set me up to die. An elf tricked my boyfriend into making a bargain that traded his free will for my life. An elf tried to bring a demon across the Break and into our world, which would have been a complete and utter disaster. I don't trust elves. And vampires, of all similarly untrustworthy creatures, helped us stop that particular elf.

Now our vampire allies have fled the ranks of the Watchtower—the initiative of humans, weres and vampires that try to protect the city from the darker races—leaving us at half-strength. Erratic half-vampires were rising in numbers, the Fey were plotting against us, and there was enough dissention among the thirteen Therian (shapeshifters) clans to keep everyone involved in the Watchtower on their toes.

I used to think my life as a Dreg Hunter was complicated. That old life is a fucking fairy tale compared to life as I know it right now.

The conference room was our War Room in the Watchtower—which isn't really a tower at all, it's more of a metaphor. We'd overtaken the skeleton of a defunct mall and revamped it to provide housing, training rooms, a cafeteria, showers, and a gymnasium. An obstacle course was under construction in one of the old department stores, and I couldn't wait to see that finished.

At the moment, work was at a stand-still while we dealt with the elf on our shelf.

Okay, so we he was sitting in a chair at one end of the conference table, surrounded by three guys with guns.

Like guns can do much against a fucking elf. Tovin plucked a bullet from the sky.

This particular elf was as calm as Tovin had been insane. Brevin, as he called himself, had been brought to us by one of my dearest friends in the world, Phineas el Chimal, an osprey-shifter who'd left us almost six weeks ago to seek out others of his kind. Brevin wasn't what anyone expected him to bring home as a souvenir of his travels.

Phineas towered over Brevin, who was about the size of a middle-schooler, skinny as a rail, with white hair and pointed ears. His sharp eyes didn't seem to miss a thing, and he'd been exceptionally polite about being asked to spend the night in one of our jail cells. Apparently Phin had explained our last encounter with an elf, and Brevin didn't seem to mind the fact that we were terrified of him.

Not that we'd ever say so out loud.

"We have quite a lot to discuss," Astrid Dane said. The co-leader of the Watchtower, she stood at the far end of the conference table with Gina Kismet on her left. Astrid was a spotted jaguar shifter, and had been leading the Watchtower since its inception. Kismet was a human, a kick-ass fighter, and had only stepped into the role when the vampires left and Adrian Baylor (another human ally and co-leader) was killed.

I didn't envy the pair their positions, and I certainly didn't want to be in charge. I was a soldier, not a captain. Point me at something and I'll fight it. Ask me to make a plan of attack, and we're probably going to be in trouble.

"We certainly do," Brevin said. His voice was deeper than expected, considering his frail shape, and carried a kind of authority found in few creatures surrounded by their mortal enemies. "Thank you for hearing me out."

"We trust Phineas's judgment," Kismet said.

I held back a smile, impressed she hadn't sprained something admitting that.

Okay, so most of we humans in the Watchtower still had trouble admitting we trusted the Therians. As Hunters, we'd been trained to distrust nonhumans on principle. Period. They were bad, we were good, end of story. Except our lives had too many shades of gray for that philosophy to stand, and now we were allies with the very creatures we once hunted.

Weird, huh?

I never expected a shifter to be my best friend and confidante, just like I never expected my lover to be half-Lupa. On my left, Wyatt Truman observed the scene without comment. Born completely human, Wyatt had been bitten and infected by a Lupa over a month ago. Lupa were wolf shifters and thought to be completely extinct, killed off by other Therians because their bites could infect a human and cause them to go insane from fever before dying a painful death. Wyatt nearly died from his bite, but in surviving, he was forever changed.

Human, Lupa, or something in between, I still loved him with my whole heart—something I never thought possible until recently.

"Brevin sought me out," Phineas said. "I believe we should give him the benefit of the doubt."

"I know you do, that's why we're here," Astrid said. "Forgive me for being leery of his motivations."

"I am not offended by your lack of trust," Brevin said. "Phineas explained what Tovin did, and I can assure you my intentions are more transparent than my kin."

"And what are your intentions?"

"Preventing Amalie from declaring all-out war on the world."

I glanced at Wyatt, unsurprised by the statement. Wyatt only had eyes for Brevin. On my other side, Marcus Dane watched the production with barely contained impatience. Astrid's brother and a fierce fighter, Marcus held an unofficial second-in-command position to our pair of leaders. He was a brawler and a force to reckon with, skin or beast, and he looked like he'd rather go tear some throats out than sit around and listen to elf stories.

Not that he was in any position to rip anyone's throat out. A few days ago he'd battled to the death with a Bengal tiger shifter named Vail, and he'd come out of it with some pretty serious gashes on his chest. The fight had left its scars on all of us though. One of my very best friends, Tybalt Monahan, had been killed during the ordeal, and we'd only buried him yesterday.

I need a fucking vacation from my life.

"We already know Amalie and the Fey are our enemies," Astrid said. "She's the one who manipulated a madman into raising Lupa pups and unleashing them on us."

"I know." Brevin turned his head to meet Wyatt's gaze. "You are no longer yourself."

Wyatt growled softly. He had a damned good reason for distrusting elves.

"Can we stay on topic, please?" Kismet asked.

"All of the Fey are not your enemies," Brevin said. "The Apothi have retreated from this fight, as have many of the Earth Guardians." Gnomes and trolls, respectively, and both formerly loyal to Amalie and the Fey Council. "I am one of three elves still alive, and we oppose Amalie."

That was news.

Two more elves in the world made me all kinds of nervous.

Brevin added, "Gargoyles are not Fey, but they oppose Amalie as well, despite leaving the city for the northern mountains."

I beat back a pang of regret at the loss of several allies. Max had been a gargoyle informant I'd used to gather intel on various Dregs, back when I was still a Hunter. He'd left the city with his fellow gargoyles ages ago, because they didn't want to get involved. He'd also saved my life when I was held and tortured by a madman named Walter Thackery. I owed Max.

A gnome named Horzt had saved Wyatt's life months ago with a healing crystal, and he'd given us a magic powder that had saved hundreds of infected vampires from a horrible death. I owed him too.

And Smedge. A bridge troll friend. Part of the earth, he'd often come up in the sandy ground beneath a train bridge. And yes, he'd saved my life once. Wyatt's, too. I owed my continued existence to so many people. I didn't know how to even begin repaying my growing debt.

"We know there are other creatures who oppose Amalie in theory," Astrid said, "but who among them is willing to stand with us openly?"

Brevin shook his head. "Very few, I am afraid. That is why I come to you now."

"You got an army up your sleeve?" I asked, breaking the promise I'd made to myself about joining in the conversation. I hated elves with a fiery rage, and Brevin was no different—not until he proved himself trustworthy. Even then I'd probably still hate him on principle.

"In a manner of speaking, yes."

"Really?"

A silent statue this entire time, Phineas shifted his weight from foot to foot. The were-osprey didn't fidget, so something was majorly up with him. He knew what Brevin was bringing to the table, and he didn't like it. I knew Phin well enough to see it in the blank expression that was working too hard to be remain neutral. It sharpened his already angular features into something fierce and feral.

And scary.

Brevin took a moment to look around the room at the people interrogating him. Astrid and Kismet, me and Wyatt, Marcus. Next to Marcus, Rufus St. James watched with the sharp care of a man used to being tricked. He sat perfectly still in his wheelchair, fingers steepled in front of his face, green eyes fixed on the elf.

No one else knew Brevin was in the Watchtower.

Sneaking him in and keeping him hidden from a mall full of Therian noses hadn't been easy, let me tell you.

Astrid crossed her arms, her long black hair pulled back in a sharp bun that made her look battle-ready. "What kind of army?" she asked.

"The kind that Amalie won't see coming," Brevin replied. "An army led by demons."

The silence in the War room was deafening.

Fuck me sideways.

As much as the idea terrified me, I stood still and listed as Brevin explained.

CHAPTER ONE

23:59

The warm body blanketing me from above snuffled. The arm around my waist pulled taut, pressing me back into Wyatt's belly. He exhaled hard, breath ruffling the hair on my cheek. Everywhere our naked skin pressed together was hot, damp, and so incredibly perfect. Even after waking up like this for the last two weeks, I still marveled at how wonderful it felt.

I never thought I'd find this kind of love and acceptance, or be so comfortable in bed with a man—especially not Wyatt.

Almost five years ago, I'd joined a secret organization called the Triads. Teams of three Hunters, lead by a Handler, we hunted and fed justice to the darker races that dwelled in the city: half-Blood vampires, goblins, rule-breaking shifters, and various other things that go bump in the night. Seven months ago, I was murdered and brought back to life, and then everything went to hell in a hard cart.

The Triads have since been destroyed, the tattered remains folded into what became the Watchtower. Wyatt had been my Handler for four years, and until my very brutal murder, my feelings for him had been pretty platonic. When I was resurrected into the recently-dead body of Chalice Frost, I found myself entertaining a whole host of attractions and feelings I'd never experienced before.

Our road toward being lovers had been long and rocky, but I'd never been happier than with Wyatt Truman.

"Dad?"

Damn it. I dragged a pillow over my head and ignored the sound of Mark's voice outside of our bedroom door.

"What is it?" Wyatt said, his voice one octave below a bellow.

"John and Peter want to go to the gym. Is that all right?"

He tensed. I didn't have to turn or ask to know why he was hesitating. The three boys were the last full-blooded Lupa in existence. Once there had been six, and ever since our discovery of the remaining brothers, Wyatt had become a surrogate father and pack leader to them. They'd also accepted me as his mate and as a quasi-mother figure.

The sudden change from single Hunter to step-mother of three teenagers had been a mind-fuck, let me tell you.

Everyone at the Watchtower knew who John, Peter and Mark were, and they knew the boys were under our protection. It still didn't stop old prejudices against Lupa from affecting the attitudes of the other Therians. Lupa had been all but eradicated because they refused to follow Assembly laws, and they infected humans for sport. While one of their dead brothers had been responsible for Wyatt's infection, neither of us blamed the three red-headed teens that had been thrust into our lives. They were desperate for love and acceptance, and I could relate to that.

Everyone deserved the chance to have a family. Even one as fucked up as ours.

"For an hour," Wyatt finally replied.

"Thanks!"

I rolled to face Wyatt, unsurprised to see apprehension lining his forehead. I smoothed my hand through his thick black hair, then down his neck to rasp against the near-permanent stubble on his cheeks and chin. He leaned into the touch, eyelids dropping down over black eyes now permanently flecked with silver.

He nuzzled my palm, his free hand tracing gentle circles on my lower back. I nudged my thigh against his groin, unsurprised to find a semi-hard on. Lupa were incredibly sexual creatures, often aroused even when nothing remotely sexy was going on. I was still getting used to it, and Wyatt constantly reminded me that just because he was sporting wood, he didn't expect to have sex. It was a thing we were still working out, a push-pull battle between his ingrained desires and his unwillingness to accidentally hurt me.

"Morning," he said.

"Good morning, hot stuff."

He rolled me under, settling between my thighs. The gentle weight of his belly pressed close to mine reminded me I was wanted and loved. So much of my past was violence and hatred. Having these moments with Wyatt was worth more than I could ever measure in words or gold. The hot length of him pressed against my core, and I lifted my knees, cradling him there. Arousal curled through me, driving away the last remnants of sleep and leaving me wanting.

"How do you feel?" he asked.

I couldn't lie to him. We'd gone at it for over an hour last night. "A little sore."

The flash of regret was there and gone quickly. He started to pull away, but I locked my ankles behind his back.

"Not that sore," I said.

"You sure?"

"Positive."

Wyatt snagged a condom from the box next to the bed. Because full-blooded Lupa bites were incredibly infectious to humans, we were careful about how we kissed and made love. And since there hadn't been a half-Lupa in centuries, no one knew if the same antigens in his blood would transfer through semen, and our on-staff doctor couldn't be sure. Wyatt wouldn't take any chances with infecting me with the Lupa virus, so we used protection every time.

I loosened my hold long enough for him to put on the condom, then pulled him inside of me. He swallowed my groan, mouth locking over mine in a searing kiss that made my toes curl and my insides ache for him. For everything we were and could ever be together. He moved in long, hard thrusts that made the bed creak and sent the frame slamming into the wall, and I didn't give a shit if our neighbors heard. We belonged to each other, and I would never be ashamed of that.

In my old life, sex had been a way to blow off steam. I hadn't cared who, as long as I got off, and some days the rougher the better. And then I was kidnapped by goblins and raped to death, and sex became something scary. Something used to hurt me. Wyatt's patience and love had turned a horror into a beautiful thing, and I loved him more every single day for what he'd given back to me.

Pleasure lashed through me, heating my blood, and I thrust up against him. Often times old fears prevented us from making love like this, with Wyatt engulfing me with his bulk, on my back. This morning I was enthralled by it. I took everything he gave me, demanding more. Sweat beaded his forehead and shoulders, and it slicked the skin between us.

I grabbed his ass and urged him on, harder, faster, to end the kind of quickie we rarely indulged in because it never felt like enough. I wanted all of him, to lick and suck and stroke, not a simple wham-bam roll in the hay. But today was the day that our lives changed, and I wanted every moment I could get with my lover.

He hiked my right leg higher, deepening his angle on each stroke. I raked my nails down his back, and he rewarded me by sucking on the hollow spot beneath my collarbone. I cried out something nonsensical. He worked a hand between us and rubbed circles over my clit, and everything went momentarily white. My entire body tightened, then relaxed, as pure pleasure washed over me. My thighs trembled from it, and I couldn't stop shaking. Not even when Wyatt plunged deeply twice more and groaned through his own orgasm. He held us together, our bodies joined by sweat and ecstasy, both of us breathing hard.

He pressed his face into my shoulder and exhaled long, deep breaths. I stroked his back with gentle fingers, enjoying the fine tremors that ran down his spine. The lovely aftershocks of his release. I kissed his temple, reveling in the fleeting perfection of the moment.

"I love you," I said.

"Love you too." He kissed my cheeks, my nose, then my lips. "So much, Evy. I love you so much and for so long."

He dumped the condom, and then pulled me back into his arms. We existed like that for a while, the real world held at bay for a bit longer.

"Are you thinking about the meeting?" I asked.

"Can't stop. You?"

"Trying hard not to think about it."

"Ignoring it won't make it go away this time."

"It never does."

I wasn't the "ignore a problem and hope it goes away" kind of girl. I'm the "kick it in the face or kill it to make it go away" kind of fighter, and I always have been. But kicking and killing wouldn't solve the problem staring us in the face, nor would it do much good at today's scheduled meeting. All I could do was wait and see what everyone else involved had to say.

"What do you think the Assembly will decide?" I asked.

"It's hard to guess at this point. They're still fighting over what Vale tried to do to the Dane family."

Tried to do meaning a coup. Each of the thirteen shifter Clans had an Elder representative on the Assembly, which met and made decisions on behalf of all of the Clans. The Felia (aka the cat shifters) Pride had come under attack by some of their own, a family of Bengals led by a man named Vale, intent on overthrowing Elder Marcellus Dane and replacing him on the Assembly. The entire thing had backfired, the bad guy was dead, and Elder Dane had officially stepped down due to health reasons. An Assembly vote a few days ago placed Astrid and Marcus's cousin Riley into Marcellus's position of Elder.

Vale's accomplices had been punished by the Assembly, but rumor was a few of the Elders had actually sided with Vale. No one was admitting to it—that I knew about—so it was difficult to determine which Clans were still Watchtower allies.

Of course, the issue went far beyond the Watchtower. If Amalie chose to go to war with the rest of the world, she wouldn't pick and choose her enemies. Every single human, Therian, vampire, and whoever else she hated at that moment would be targeted by her minions.

I had no idea how fairies and sprites went to war, and I had no desire whatsoever to find out.

"We should get up," I said. "The meeting is in three hours."

Wyatt grumbled, but released me from his iron grip.

We were in some of the newest housing in the Watchtower. Most of the single members lived in dormitory style housing built in an old store front. A larger store across the corridor had been turned into something more like multi-room apartments. We had one with two bedrooms that shared a living room type space, but without the traditional kitchen area. We did have a bathroom space to share with all five of us.

Yeah, three teenage boys shared one room.

I'd already declared I was never cleaning that room. Ever.

I'm a warrior, not a maid.

The boys were gone by the time we were showered, dressed, and deemed ourselves presentable to the rest of the our coworkers. Wyatt wore his familiar uniform of black jeans and a black t-shirt. With his black hair, scruff and olive skin, the picture was drool-worthy, and he was all mine. I stuck to jeans and a long-sleeve tee, with a corduroy jacket, now that the fall weather was inching into winter.

The meeting would happen at ten a.m. in the War room, so we had time to hit the cafeteria. My stomach was tight and squirrely with nerves, and it didn't settle at the crowd already filling the spacious eating area. Even those who patrolled at night and slept during the day were up, the air full of anxiety and curiosity.

I grabbed a plain bagel and bottle of water, while Wyatt piled his plate high with food of all kinds. His half-

Lupa nature had practically doubled his metabolism, which meant he was hungry almost all of the time. I wasn't complaining about the way his arms and abs were cut to perfection, but the frequent eating made me jealous.

Wyatt nudged my hip, then angled his head. I followed his general direction to a table near the back, farther away from the bulk of the crowd. Gina Kismet, Marcus Dane, and Milo Gant sat there alone, the three of them as serious as I'd ever seen them. Seeing Milo eating in the cafeteria made my heart kick in a happy way.

Not quite two weeks ago, Milo had been nearly beaten to death by Vale in an attempt to make Marcus give up important security information. Milo had held on, never letting Vale break him, but he'd been left with serious injuries to his back and legs—swelling that had taken days to go down, bruises that still painted his skin, and pain that would be a long time fading. Tybalt and Milo had been brothers to me, and I couldn't have stood losing them both. I was barely handling Tybalt's death.

The walker Milo used for long-distance hobbling stood nearby, and he looked up with a bright smile when he saw me and Wyatt heading in his direction. "Hey, guys."

I plunked down across from him. "What's shaking, gimpy?"

"Fuck you," Milo said with a grin.

"Milo's progress has increased tremendously in the last few days," Marcus said. He tended to take my teasing a bit too seriously, but the big werecat was also seriously overprotective of Milo. I still wasn't sure if the pair was technically a couple, but they gave off serious "I want you" vibes when they were together.

Things probably would have progressed a lot faster if Vale hadn't decided to make Milo a human punching bag. I bristled briefly at the memories of Milo's torture, then shoved them down deep where they wouldn't bother me today. No regrets, no past issues. Today was about taking back our future, no matter what.

"I don't have to stay in the infirmary anymore," Milo said. "I can go back to the dorms tonight."

Marcus's expression was difficult to decipher. Something between pleasure and a silent reassurance that he wouldn't be alone, no matter what dorm he went back to. I liked knowing Marcus was around to take care of Milo. They both needed someone.

"That's fabulous news, pal." I reached over the table to ruffle his hair, because it would bother him. He stuck his tongue out, and I laughed.

"Wish I could be at the meeting with you guys today," Milo added.

"It's a pretty tight guest list."

"And for good reason," Marcus added. "Many Elders will be present, as well as other leaders. Security will extra important given the nature of the meeting."

"And they don't need a useless guard hanging around."

"You are far from useless."

"He's always good for a sarcastic comment," I said.

Milo flipped me off.

Wyatt ate in silence, as he often did around any of the Felia. Lupa and Felia were mortal enemies, ingrained in their DNA or something like that. From the moment he was infected and became aware of his surroundings again, Wyatt had snarled and snapped at Marcus specifically. To the other Felia to a lesser degree. Wyatt was learning to control himself, but he too frequently struggled to maintain his humanity.

Some days I wondered if the Lupa blood in his system was going to take away what was left of the man.

I hope not. I love him too much to let him go.

"Gina says the obstacle course will be back on schedule soon," Milo said. "I can't wait to run it and kick your ass."

I snickered. "Dream on, Gant."

"Hey, I told you I'd kick your *and* Tybalt's asses." His smile faltered, fractured by grief. Tybalt had been Milo's best friend and part of his Triad for almost two years, and the wound was still fresh. He'd lost a brother, too.

"We all miss him," Marcus said.

Milo shrugged and picked at the remnants of his breakfast.

One day we'd be able to talk about our lost friends without feeling such a thick, blanket of grief. I hoped.

My phone chimed with a text. **Ops. 911.**

Great. Emergency first thing in the morning. No one else at the table had gotten the message, but that didn't stop Wyatt from grabbing a handful of sausage links and following me.

The entire mall was in the shape of a big, square-ish U. The cafeteria sat at one corner of the top of the U, with Operations near the center of the top. It was a short walk down the corridor, which was thick with

Watchtower members. Rumors about today's big meet-up had spread, and everyone wanted to see who'd show.

I entered Operations, which was the heart and soul of our organization. Besides the War Room, it also housed a bank of computers and large screens that projected pretty much anything we needed to see. Rufus oversaw most of Ops, because he had the most computer skills among the senior staff. Milo could probably give him a run for his figurative money, but Milo preferred staying in the field to being stuck behind a desk.

Given his wheelchair, Rufus didn't have much choice in the matter.

Rufus looked up from his computer terminal, his expectant look melting into a frown. "Who invited you?"

Wyatt growled. "I invited myself."

"Obviously."

I shrugged. "I tried a leash, but he keeps breaking loose."

"You really don't need to shadow her everywhere, Wyatt," Rufus said.

"I know that," Wyatt replied.

"Right." He turned his attention back to me, the one he had summoned. "It's about the Frosts."

"What did they do now?" Lori and Stephen Frost were the biological parents of the body in which I was currently residing. While I'd absorbed some of Chalice's memories and sensory perceptions, I didn't know them as my parents. My parents were an unknown deadbeat and a drunken whore.

For a while, they'd sat by while Chalice didn't contact them for more than six months. Last week they'd finally gone on the news trying to find their missing daughter, and a private detective tricked me into meeting with them. We'd brought them back to the Watchtower for their own good, and neither one of them had taken the news about my true nature well—or the fact that shapeshifters, gremlins, and other assorted creatures actually did exist.

Not well at all.

Astrid had ordered them kept here until further notice, and I'd refused to visit them for the last week. I had too much to do and no patience to deal with them.

"Astrid doesn't want them locked up indefinitely, and I agree that it's cruel," Rufus said. "Their daughter is dead, and they deserve a chance to grieve for her."

I crossed my arms. "And what the hell am I supposed to do about it?"

"Talk to them again."

"And say what? Stephen thinks I'm possessed or something. They want me in therapy."

"I could talk to them," Wyatt said.

"No way," I replied. "You're about as subtle as a two-by-four to the head."

"You're no diplomat yourself, Evy."

Okay, so he had me there. "If I honestly thought anything I had to say would make a difference, I'd go talk to them. I'm not their daughter. All they see when they look at me is Chalice. I'm never going to make them believe I'm Evy Stone."

"We've been holding them prisoner for over a week," Rufus said. "We can't keep them here forever. They have lives to go back to. Sooner or later someone is going to start missing them."

"How do you know they haven't already?"

He pointed to his computer. "I've been sending emails on their behalf to coworkers and other relatives, so no one calls in another missing persons report."

"Oh." That was pretty fucking smart of him.

"Yeah, oh."

"Stone!" Astrid's voice boomed across Ops.

"I didn't do it," I said as I turned.

She faltered, then understood the joke. "I need a quick errand."

"How quick? The meeting starts in two hours."

"Your errand should take you less than an hour."

"To do what?"

"Pick up something that will help your parents forget they ever saw you."

Okey dokey.

CHAPTER TWO

22:25

Turns out the little thing that Astrid needed me to run out and grab was less of a grabby thing and more like a threatening thing. She gave me the address of a mage named Adolpho, who ran a small antiques store on the southwestern side of the city. And when I say small, you'd drive right past it if you didn't know to look for it, nestled among a dozen boarded up store fronts in a little used part of the neighborhood.

Wyatt being Wyatt insisted on coming with me to do my errand. Since I didn't technically have a drivers license, nor had I ever been taught to drive properly, he took Alpha joy in driving us to the mage's shop. Few other cars passed us on the street, and no one was parked in front of the papered over front doors with the tiny "Collectibles" sign in the window.

He scented the air as we stepped out of the Jeep, as was his new habit. The Lupa infection had heightened his senses of smell, hearing and taste, and he was still learning how to use those to his advantage. The smell thing was super useful, considering goblins stank like stale sea water, and he once described a half-Blood as "ass and congealed blood."

Gross as hell, but such was our life.

Despite the drizzling rain, the street still smelled like old urine and gasoline, and the combination turned my stomach. The shop had a Closed sign hanging in it. I banged my first on the glass plates anyway, uncertain if Adolpho lived near, above, or in his supposed collectible shop. Wyatt tilted his head.

"Footsteps," he whispered.

"Oh joy."

Plastic blinds parted and a bright green eye appeared, the rest of his face obscured by the door. The eye shifted to take us both in, then the blinds dropped. Nothing.

"Astrid Dane sent me," I said, hoping that would work in the vein of "Open sesame."

I'll be damned if the door lock didn't turn. He opened it with the chain still attached. "For what purpose?" the man asked.

"You tell me. She said I had to come here and fetch something."

He squinted. "She said she would send someone she trusted."

Okay, One-Eyed-Mage was getting on my nerves. "She does trust me. I trust her, too, which is why I didn't ask what I was picking up. As long as it isn't poisonous or explodable, I don't really give a flying fuck."

"I don't know…"

Wyatt growled. "You remember Brutus?"

Adolpho's eye widened. "Yes. Sorry." The door shut, the chain slid, and then it was open again. Wider this time. Adolpho was a big, barrel of a man with no hair, a scraggly gray beard, and only one eye. The left socket was puckered and empty. "My apologies, come inside."

The shop reeked of herbs that blended together into one indistinguishable odor, mixed with the musty smell of a closed-in space. The first few shelves nearest the door were filled with rusty trinkets and cloudy pieces of glassware. Beyond it was a wall, and through a thick panel of beaded curtains was a setup very much like an ancient apothecary shop. A wall of wooden drawers, many no wider than a credit card, some as big as a shoe box, each labeled in a language that I couldn't read.

It reminded me of Old World Teas and its owner Brutus, the last mage we'd ousted for working with the sprites. Adolpho seemed much more high-strung, less likely to be pulling the whole double-agent thing that Brutus had pulled with Wyatt for years.

I wiped rainwater off my arms and face. Wyatt didn't seem to notice the droplets trickling down his cheeks from his hair.

Adolpho lifted a ring of ancient-looking keys out from beneath his baggy shirt. He fitted one into a drawer and slid it open. He removed a brown leather pouch with a drawstring. "This is what Astrid asked for," he said, dangling the pouch from two fingers. "Steep it in two cups of boiled water for at least five minutes, and then make them each drink half."

I snagged the pouch and received a waft of something not unlike peppermint. "What's it do?"

"It does as Astrid required."

That told me exactly nothing. "Which is what?"

He shook his head. "You'll have to inquire with her. I've done as she asked."

Wyatt took a step forward, allowing silver to rise up and fill his eyes. He growled softly, an intense sound that made Adolpho back into a cabinet with a yelp. "Don't play word games, mage."

Adolpho gulped hard, his Adam's apple bobbing. "She required a potion that muddled human memories and she needs enough for two."

The Frosts. "How does it muddle memories?" I asked.

"They will be confused about the events of the last month or so, as though coming around from a blackout drunk."

Astrid had ordered magic used on the Frosts to make them forget they'd ever found me, or that I'd told them who I really was.

Shit, fuck and hell.

While removing their memories was a much better solution than keeping them locked up forever, I didn't like that Astrid had gone behind my back. I didn't like that she was using a mage to create an herbal spell that would make them fuzzy on "a month or so" of time. What if it was longer? What if it didn't work? What if Lori Frost woke up and she'd turned into a frog?

Stranger things have happened in this fucking city.

"If the herbs aren't applied properly, what could happen?" I asked.

"Full memory loss."

"Are the memories recoverable if that happens?"

"No, so apply wisely, child."

I hated being called child. "Okay, thanks for this."

Adolpho nodded. "Tell Astrid my debt is repaid."

"Yeah, sure."

The light rain had become a steady downpour by the time we got back to the car. My t-shirt clung to my skin. I turned on the heater to try and dry us both out a little bit.

"Astrid wants those herbs for the Frosts, doesn't she?" Wyatt asked.

"I have no doubt." I tapped my fingers against the dash. "Shit, Wyatt, what if something goes wrong?"

"You genuinely care?"

"Of course I do." From anyone but Wyatt, that question would have come across as condescending. He was truly curious. "They aren't my parents in the sense that I was raised by them, but they raised this body. They genuinely loved their daughter. I have a sense of connection, and I don't want to see them hurt."

"I understand that."

I stroked the smooth leather pouch, too aware of the dangerous herbs inside it. "Astrid has to know I'd ask what this does, and she'll know I won't like it."

"Maybe she expected you to balk, and this is her way of giving you a push."

"A push where?"

"A push into doing something about the Frosts."

"Why are they my responsibility? I didn't ask to get resurrected into their daughter. I didn't ask them to come here looking for her, and I certainly didn't ask for O'Reilly to introduce me to them. Nor did I ask for Vale to fucking kidnap them and put them right into the middle of this mess."

Wyatt held up his hands in a gesture of surrender. "I know all of that, Evy. In some ways, your being inside of their daughter is my fault."

"How do you figure?"

"I initiated the resurrection spell."

"Yeah, well, you had no idea I'd resurrect into a body that had a connection to the Break, rather than the dead Hunter you'd prepared for me." That particular wrinkle had been a bonus for us, because me resurrecting somewhere other than in the expected place had put the first wrinkle into Tovin's plan for bringing a demon across the Break—the magical barrier between this world and the one where dark creatures had been banished long ago.

Breaks existed all over the city, and humans went about their days unaware of them. But if a human is born over a Break, they have a connection to it which often leads to a Gift of some sort. Wyatt was Gifted. He could summon inanimate, inorganic materials into his hand from a decent distance—a Gift he was still learning to control post-Lupa infection. My new Gift was the ability to transport from one location to another. I could go through solid objects, but it hurt like a motherfucker, so I didn't like doing that. The talent had saved my life more than once these last six months, and it had been another fantastic foil to Tovin's plan.

Did I mention my other handy ability to rapidly heal? That came courtesy of the resurrection spell. I'd have been dead ten times over without it.

"You don't get to take responsibility for this," I said. "There's no one person at fault for this mess."

Wyatt grunted. "Seems to me the entire mess can be traced directly back to Tovin's first manipulations."

"Maybe. Then we'll blame the elf. No more self-blame. Understood?"

He leaned in closer, eyes narrowing. "Have I told you lately you're really hot when you give me orders?"

"Not lately, no." The gleam in his eyes was all too familiar, and we had work yet to do. "Down boy."

He grinned, and my heart skipped.

Then my phone screeched with a general alert text, Wyatt's following an instant later. I checked the message.

Kismet: **Backup ASAP. Union Street Salvage.**

"That's only a few blocks from here," Wyatt said.

"I'll call it in."

He made the turn. We'd both lived in this city our entire lives, and we knew every single street and side road.

Gina Kismet led Quad Four, and they were on patrol this morning. She worked alongside Shelby, an Ursia who shifted into a big-ass polar bear, and Kyle, a Cania dingo-shifter. The other person on their team had been Tybalt, and they'd yet to replace him in what were typically quads of two humans and two Therians. The problem was we didn't have any more trained humans to fold into the quad, and Astrid liked to keep the human-to-Therian ratio balanced because it fostered tolerance or something like that.

All I cared about was the team needed backup.

I let Ops know that we were responding to the call. The salvage yard was easy to find, its massive acreage surrounded by a metal fence topped with razor wire. The east side hadn't been my stomping grounds as a Hunter, but I'd heard a few stories about tracking Halfies through the salvage yard for hours on end.

Lucky for us the place was owned and operated by a family of Prosi who were human-friendly and pro-Watchtower. A big, fenced-in area full of places to climb, jump and swing on seemed pretty fitting for people who shifted in lemurs and bushbabies.

The entrance was off the corner of Union Street and a dirt road to nowhere, marking the end of city limits. Union itself trailed off into undeveloped land that eventually became part of the forested mountains surrounding the city. A rain-soaked, rail-thin man in denim coveralls held open a chain-link rolling fence for us without even asking for ID, then promptly shut it with himself on the outside.

Prosi weren't known for their amazing fighting skills.

Past a dingy trailer marked Office, dirt trails ran off in three different directions. Wyatt stuck his head out the window and sniffed. How he could smell anything over the stink of oil fuel and engine grease was beyond me, but eventually he took the center road. We trundled past hundreds of different kinds of cars, trucks, vans, motorcycles, and heaps of other metals. Salvaged parts of refrigerators, ovens, and all kinds of machinery was piled in no discernible way, but I guessed it made sense to the owners.

A goblin male darted out in front of the car and leapt onto the hood an instant before we'd have smashed into it. Wyatt hit the brakes, but the fucking thing grabbed onto the windshield wipers. It peered in at us, its red eyes glimmering with bloodlust. Oily black skin glistened in the rain. Most of the goblin warriors I'd fought wore loincloths. This fucker was totally naked and there was no hiding how much it was enjoying the fight.

I fought back the very real urge to vomit. Months had passed, and I had a completely different body than the one tortured to death by goblins, but some things never left you.

The goblin hissed, showing off rows of razor teeth.

Wyatt stuck his left hand out the open window and shot the thing in the head. Gore splattered the car hood.

"Guess we found the fight," I said.

We ditched the car. I hadn't left the Watchtower with anything on me except a serrated knife in my boot, so I grabbed a few more toys out of the trunk—two Glocks, a machete, and some extra rounds. Wyatt stuck with his single pistol, probably intending to bi-shift at some point so he could do more damage.

A roaring sound that could only be angry bear-Shelby rattled the tin roofing near the car. We bolted in that direction, splashing through mud puddles on our way to the main event. A goblin sailed overhead, its mangled body dead before it smashed into something out of sight.

It's going to be that kind of fight.

The odds were three to several dozen, so I jumped in the machete and cleaved through the shoulder of the nearest goblin. It screeched and yanked away, bleeding fuchsia all over itself as it stumbled into a friend. Bear-Shelby was going to town near a roofless school bus, batting at the goblins like he was playing a life-sized game of whack-a-mole.

Kyle hadn't shifted, so he and Kismet were going hand-to-hand. Both were bleeding, but I couldn't stop and assess injuries. The machete helped me thin out the horde a bit. Behind me, Wyatt roared. A hulking shadow and the squeal of several goblins told me he'd bi-shifted. Since he wasn't full Lupa, he couldn't shift completely into a wolf. He could, however, get taller, more muscular, grown insane claws on both hands, and reshape his face into something genuinely grotesque on a human being.

He was truly a monster in that form—nothing sexy about it. But he was also a formidable fighter, and we needed that in our corner.

"They keep coming," Kismet yelled over the battle roar and the rain.

I could see that. For every two I dropped, three more seemed to take their places. "From where?"

"No idea."

One of them jumped onto my back from behind. Short arms circled my neck while clawed fingers sunk into my shoulders. Teeth scraped at the my left ear and cut my scalp.

Oh hell no.

I slammed backward into the nearest hard surface. The goblin wheezed and its arms loosened. Another hard smash and it let go. I pivoted and kicked it right in the groin. It squealed, and then died when I ran it through with the machete.

Two more hit me from the side, and we all went tumbling into a puddle. Too close for the blade, I dropped it in favor of smashing their skulls together. Teeth broke and blood spurted. The awful stink of seawater rose over the other scents around me. My gut twisted. I used to take great pleasure in killing monsters like this. Once it had been fun.

Now it was a fucking responsibility.

"Gina!"

I rolled onto my knees, fingers curling around the hilt of my abandoned machete. Kyle and Kismet were separated by a cluster of goblins that seemed to be doing their best to herd Kismet away from the battle. She punched, kicked, and slashed at them with a shiny pair of butterfly swords she'd been training to use, but the goblins were overwhelming her.

Goblin warriors were only about four feet tall, but they were strong, they were dumb, and they fucked anything with a hole, including corpses. I'd experienced the agony of a goblin's hooked penis, and I'd seen too many other mutilated human victims, both male and female.

I launched at them. On my third stride, I went sideways into a car door with a wall of goblins pressing down on me. Teeth snapped at my arms and face, scraping skin and drawing blood that the rain washed away. The stench of them filled my nose. Clawed fingers ripped at my shirt.

Bitter fury rose up like bile and came out on a long scream. I swung hard with the machete. Goblin squeals were my reward, so I did it again. Blood splattered. One of them grabbed my hair and yanked my head back, exposing my throat. Sharp teeth flashed.

Wyatt snarled and smacked the goblin away. He batted a few more hard enough to snap their necks. I hacked off various body parts on my way out of the pileup. My shirt was torn, my throat and arms stung from a lot of small wounds, and I could still feel their hands on my body.

None of that fucking mattered, because Kismet was gone.

Kyle yelped. Wyatt charged off to help him.

I ran in the direction I'd seen the goblins herding Kismet, overtaking them only a few yards down a narrow path between piles of broken bricks and cement blocks. They'd apparently given up on persuasion and had lifted her up into the air like some kind of offering to the gods. She was struggling like a champ and cussing them left and right.

"Hey, shitheads!"

Some of them turned and hissed. None of them attacked, which was what I'd hoped for, so I took the party to them. No fucking way were they carting Kismet off to become their latest plaything.

I went in low, aiming for kneecaps so I didn't accidentally take a chunk out of my friend. Bones shattered. Flesh tore. Blood spurted. I moved without cataloguing any of it, aware only of my enemies and the need to beat them. My arms ached but it didn't matter.

Palms slapped down on both of my ears, and everything went gray. My equilibrium shattered all to hell, and I fell to my knees with a jolt up my spine.

Fucker boxed my ears.

I blinked hard through the rain, aware of lots of small legs carrying my enemies away from me. I fumbled for one of the Glocks, fell flat to my chest in the mud, and opened fire. Bullets struck flesh. Goblins screamed. Faltered. Fell.

The goblin who'd boxed my ears clamped its mouth down on my wrist. Fire lashed up my arm, right to my shoulder. I transferred the gun to my left hand, and then shot the thing between the eyes. Seawater blood splattered me in the face. Teeth scored my arm as the body fell, leaving pencil-thick gouges down the length of it.

Dizzy and nauseated, I hauled ass to my feet. Pocketed the gun for now and scooped the machete back up.

Somewhere behind me a big cat cried out in anger. More backup.

"A little help!" I shouted.

I followed small rivers of fuchsia past the piles of bricks, deeper into the salvage yard. The cars and whatnot got rustier and dirtier the farther back I trailed the goblins. Small trees and bushes had come to life inside some of the husks. I couldn't exactly be stealthy about tracking them with my wet boots squishing into mud with every step, so I went for speed instead.

Kismet screamed.

"Gina!"

A goblin jumped from the shell of an old pickup truck, mouth open, hands extended. I took its fucking head off before it could blink, and I kept running.

The horde had stopped where the ground dipped down to the perimeter fence. A dozen small trees had grown up near the fence, and piles of old shingles had gone to rot nearby. I couldn't see Kismet for their moving bodies, so I pulled both guns and opened fire on anything that wasn't human.

Two, six, twelve, twenty of them fell dead, and the final few ran toward the trees. I hit one on the back, and down it went. The other two I let go.

Kismet sat up from beneath the pile of bodies, her skin smeared in gore. Red blood mixed with fuchsia in a graphic war paint that was all the more hideous due to the fact that her shirt was gone. She stared at me with wide eyes, one hand stanching blood from someplace on her neck. I picked a path over the bodies and squatted in front of her.

"You with me?" I asked.

"Yeah." She shook herself all over. "Jesus Christ. Did that really happen?"

"Almost happened." I helped her stand up. "You hurt anywhere?"

"Superficial."

She was bleeding from at least a dozen cuts and standing there topless, but her jeans seemed intact so I wasn't going to question her on her definition of the word superficial. She finally seemed to notice the topless thing and wrapped her arms around her breasts.

A lioness leapt into the mess from somewhere above us. She sniffed at us, then followed her nose down toward the trees and fence. The small dark patch on her left shoulder was the only way I knew that was Lynn Neil.

"Evy?" Wyatt had undone his bi-shift, which left his shirt sleeves stretched out and torn in a few places. He took one look at Kismet and slipped his shirt off. "What the hell happened?"

"The goblins were trying to take Gina with them," I said.

His dark gaze went deadly.

"Evy was pretty badass with that machete," Kismet said as she tugged on the too big shirt. "You've been practicing."

"They weren't taking you." I wouldn't wish that kind of fate on my worst enemy, let alone allow it to happen to a friend.

"Why did they want me, though?"

"Something tells me they would have happily carted off anyone who was human."

"What happened?" Wyatt asked.

"We were doing a simple patrol of the area when we got a call about a possible goblin sighting out here," Gine said, "so we checked it out. We were attacked, and we called for backup. You guys came. End of story."

"Why does this whole thing feel like a setup?" I asked.

"Because it is," Kyle said.

He approached with naked Shelby behind him—clothing became problematic when it came to shapeshifting—and flanked by humans Carly and Oliver.

They were part of a quad with Lynn and an Equi named Nestor, who was the only person MIA.

"How do you know it was a setup?" Kismet asked.

"The goblins left us a present a few rows back. Nestor's guarding it."

The only presents goblins ever left behind were dead bodies.

"Where's Lynn?" Carly asked.

I jacked a thumb over my shoulder. "Sniffing down around the fence. It's where the goblins were heading. We'll check out the present if you guys want to investigate that." It wasn't a question so much as a polite order, and no one contradicted me.

Wyatt hovered close to Kismet on the walk back. Shelby seemed to know where Nestor was, so Kyle and I followed him, the other pair behind us. Wyatt and Kismet had been friends for more than ten years, and they had this brother/sister love between them. He knew she was freaked out by what had just happened—as freaked out as Kismet ever got around other people—and he was doing his silent supportive thing.

Nestor was a tall fellow, with a long face and dark hair—both things typical of his Clan. He was a zebra shifter and somewhat new to the Watchtower. He stood with his arms crossed, at attention in front of an old VW bus. "It's gory," he said.

Definitely new. "My entire adult life has been one gorefest after another," I said. "Bring it on."

He stepped aside.

I smelled it first—the ripe odors of blood and meat left in the sun too long. The interior of the bus had been stripped of all furnishings, leaving a shell that was coated in blood. Some of it had been washed off by the rain through the windows and puddled on the floor with the various parts of someone's body. Male, female, I wasn't sure. The pieces were too small. My stomach churned, and I stepped back before I got sick all over Nestor.

Wyatt stuck his head in the open door. "Male, not freshly killed. I suspect the dismemberment happened post-mortem."

I wasn't about to ask how he knew that.

"There's a note." He turned around clutching a wet sheet of paper, his expression grim.

"What's it say?" Kismet asked when I didn't.

His black eyes flashed silver. "Stone or more. Which will die?"

"Fuck me." My gut rolled. The goblins knew I was alive.

CHAPTER THREE

21:05

"Nessa, again?" Kismet asked.

"Has to be," I replied.

Goblin societies are matriarchal, one female queen born for every thousand or so males. Each queen has her own horde of male warriors, which could number up into the hundreds, and for the most part they lived in the sewers beneath the city. Several months ago, I'd very happily killed the queen who'd tortured me to death. Recently though, another queen decided she didn't like me doing that, and she had upped her horde's visibility in the city. Dead bodies were piling up.

We had another John Doe to thank Nessa for.

One of these days I'd like to go a solid week without someone wanting me dead.

"Do you think Nessa was trying to draw you out?" Kismet asked. "And her idiot warriors nabbed me by mistake?"

I shook my head. "No, I think she wanted her boys to grab any human I work with so she could send me a personal message. Bonus points if they're someone close to me."

She made a face.

"So either you turn yourself over to the goblins, or this Nessa keeps unleashing her horde on humans?" Shelby said. "Is this one of those greater good conundrums?"

"No." Wyatt turned on Shelby with a furious snarl that startled even me. "She isn't going back to the goblins. Period."

I grabbed Wyatt's wrist and squeezed, half-afraid he'd take a swing at the naked were-bear. I doubted Wyatt would ever be able to forget those moments when I was found in that old train station, broken and dying. We both knew what turning myself over would mean, and no way in fuck was I that stupid. I'd sooner take a header off the Lincoln Street Bridge.

"No one's going anywhere right this minute," I said. "Except for those of us heading home."

"I vote home," Kismet said. "I need a shower."

"You need to see Dr. Vansis, too. You're covered in cuts, and goblins aren't exactly sanitary."

"You have as many as I do."

I probably did. "Yeah, well, I heal a lot faster than you."

She frowned, but didn't argue further.

"How are you three for injuries?" I asked the guys, who all seemed amused by our banter.

Shelby had a few scrapes, while Kyle's arms and legs looked as bad as mine felt. We trekked back to the car. I stuffed myself into the backseat with Kismet and Kyle so the two bigger guys could make use of the front. Shelby gave a brief phone report to someone in Ops while Wyatt drove us home.

Kismet was shivering by the time we got back to the Watchtower. I rustled an emergency blanket out of the trunk. She pulled it tight around her shoulders. Instinct kept me close while we walked to the infirmary, our party leaving a trail of bloody footprints in our wake.

Not exactly a rare occurrence around here.

Phineas, Astrid and Dr. Vansis were waiting for us in the infirmary. For all that he shifted into a giant grizzly bear, Dr. Vansis often reminded me of a nerdy science professor. Slim, short multi-hued hair that all Ursia shared, and a penchant for being abrupt and clinical. But he was a damned good doctor, even when dealing with human physiology.

"I send you on one errand," Astrid said with a huff.

"It's not my fault." I pointed at Kismet. "She called for backup. We responded."

"Good thing they did, too," Kismet said. "I don't think I've ever seen so many goblins attacking in broad daylight."

"Broad rain light."

"Whatever."

"Who is bleeding the most?" Dr. Vansis asked.

I pointed at Kyle and Kismet. "Take them."

He led them off to cubicles to do his doctor thing.

Phineas handed me a towel. "You are impressively injured yourself, Evangeline."

"Thanks. Goddamn goblins." I rubbed the towel through my hair out of habit, surprised to find it nearly dry. Score for the short cut. Made tending it ten times simpler than when it was long and wavy.

Wyatt explained what had happened in greater detail, with myself and Shelby chiming in with occasional details. He'd nearly finished the story when Astrid's phone rang.

"It's Carly," she said as she answered. "You're on speaker."

"We found another entrance to the sewers," Carly said, her voice tinny over the speaker phone. "Down by the trees where Stone saw some of the goblins disappear. It's well hidden, and it doesn't appear to be used very often. We found evidence of human blood near the entrance, but no remains."

"I think the remains are in a VW bus," I said.

"I want your team to stay there and guard that entrance," Astrid said. "Nothing comes in or out until further notice."

"Understood," Carly replied. "How are our people?"

"Alive and accounted for. I'll be in touch." Astrid switched off the phone, then pinched the bridge of her nose. "Okay, so the goblins are threatening to keep killing until they get Stone. We are obviously not turning her over to them. Options?"

"I'm all for napalming the sewers," I said, "but you guys keep telling me that it's impractical."

"The Watchtower Initiative is here to keep the peace, not impose blanket genocide."

"Right, only Therians get to declare genocide on someone they don't like."

Astrid's lips pulled back. I shouldn't have been goading her by mentioning the centuries old destruction of the Lupa Clan, but my brain to mouth censor was usually fried after a life-and-death fight.

Ever the rational one, Phineas steered me to the far side of the waiting room where he plunked me down into a chair. "I know you'll heal, but those wounds should be cleaned."

"So I'll take a shower." I was damp, exhausted, and very cranky. All of my cuts and gashes were making themselves known. Dealing with antiseptic swabs was not on my list of things to do in the immediate future.

Phineas possessed the uncanny ability to make me feel like a chastised child with only the arch of one slender eyebrow. He looked up. "Will you deal with her, please?"

Wyatt sat in the chair next to me and put a possessive hand on my knee. "I'll make sure she takes care of herself."

"She'll make sure she takes care of her own damned self," I said. I appreciated the love, but the hovering was starting to grate. "I could have gone straight to take a shower and let my unnatural healing power do its thing, but no, Alpha dude over here insisted the Infirmary."

Phin's lips twitched. "She does have a good point."

"Thank you."

"Don't encourage her," Wyatt said.

"Bite my blood soaked ass, Truman. You know what? I'm going to take that shower. Whatever cuts and gashes are still around when I'm done can be looked over by the doc."

I stalked out of the Infirmary, sore and tired and kind of annoyed. Not really at Wyatt or Phineas. Mostly at the goblins. Nessa in particular, who'd decided to make it her mission to see me dead again, no matter how many innocents paid the price. All of my friends at the Watchtower were targets. The only other ally of mine still bopping around the city unprotected was a private investigator named James Reilly, who'd some me some favors lately. He knew about the city's supernatural underbelly. He knew how high the stakes were.

Bringing him in for his protection might not be a bad idea. God only knew how the goblins got their information, and we'd been seen together in public more than once. He didn't deserve to get caught up in my ever-present drama.

Wyatt shocked the hell out of me by not immediately landing on my heels. Probably saved himself some blue balls for a while, too. I didn't need to be coddled, damn it, and I wasn't the one who'd nearly been carted off to become a goblin horde's newest plaything. Kismet needed their support. I needed a fucking shower.

At the angle in the corridor that would lead me to the apartments, I nearly ran Milo down. His walker was the only thing that saved us from a full-on collision, but I hit it hard enough to send him reeling. I grabbed his shirt collar and tugged, keeping him upright. Marcus would skin me if Milo fell and hurt himself.

"Hey, have you seen Gina?" he asked. "I keep hearing things, but no one seems to really know what happened on her patrol."

"Gina's fine. She's in the infirmary getting a bunch of goblin cuts looked at but she's fine."

Kind of.

He narrowed his eyes at me. I knew that expression well enough by now. "Tell me what happened."

I did, leaving out the goriest of the details. Milo had fought as many goblins as I had. He knew how they fought and how disgustingly they died. When I got to the part about them dragging Kismet off, his face got hard. Furious. Behind it was something else kind of like grief. Then the fury and grief merged into determination. "She's in the infirmary?"

"Yes, and she's not alone," I said. "Wyatt, Phin and Astrid are all there." It finally hit me that for the first time in the last couple of days, Milo was missing his shadow. "Where's your other half?"

"He said he'd look into what happened today, but I got impatient waiting."

"Marcus will have kittens if he finds out you're wandering around alone."

Milo snickered. "Yeah, well, I'm a big boy and I can hobble around without assistance, thank you very much. And if Gina was—I need to talk to her. Make sure she's okay."

Okay, I was missing a piece of the puzzle. A few days ago, Gina had had an uncharacteristic moment of weakness and confided in me about her past. Only a snippet, but enough to know that she'd suffered as a teenage runaway who put her trust into an older man. A man who said he'd take care of her and abused her in ways that I hadn't brought myself to ask about. We each had our personal demons, and we didn't need to compare notes to know the pain was genuine.

She'd also told me I was the only living person who knew about that man—unless she'd confided in Milo in the past few days, which was unlikely given their combined mental states. Both grieving the loss of a brother in arms.

Milo knew about something else.

"What happened to her?" I asked, surprising myself with the depth of my concern over a woman who'd once tried to kill me on orders from her former bosses.

He glanced around, but the few residents coming and going weren't paying us any real attention. "You remember Felix's first night on the Triad, when Gina was brought into the ER because she'd been seriously beaten by some asshole frat boys in the parking lot of our apartment building?"

I cast about for those memories, roughly two and a half years ago. Wyatt had been out of his mind with worry and unable to keep Gina's Hunter Lucas Moore from picking and sniping at my Triad. I'd always had a short temper, but it was far worse before my death and resurrection—bad enough that my late Triad partner Jesse had once marveled I managed to last four whole years.

"Sure I do," I said. "Lucas and I ended up in a bit of a scuffle that our respective Triad partners broke up. But you weren't even a Hunter yet when all that happened."

"I know. Felix and Tybalt told me about it later, because my first night I made a comment about Tybalt walking Gina to her car."

Somehow that didn't surprise me. Trauma changed a person. Even someone as strong as Gina Kismet. Eventually the cops tracked down the three assholes who assaulted her, and—*fuck me.*

Milo must have seen my thought process in my expression, because he held up a staying hand. "Hold on, before you leap to conclusions."

Me? Never. "Then what?"

He leaned forward. "They tried to rape her that night, but they didn't. Tybalt and Lucas and Felix, they stopped it before it got that far, but…"

"I get it." Kismet had still felt that fear, that sense of horror knowing that she was about to be violated. Getting dragged toward a tunnel by a horde of goblins had likely put her right back in that parking lot. "Go talk to her then."

"Thanks. Where are you headed?"

I glance down at my blood-splattered clothes, then quirk an eyebrow at him.

Milo grinned. "Dumb question. How many did you get?"

"Not nearly enough."

Never enough, not until all of them were dead.

"You okay?" he asked, all serious again.

"I think so. Never thought I'd say this, but I'm getting tired of killing. One of these days, Milo, I swear to Christ I want the biggest decision I have to make is which fruity drink a server will bring to me on a tropical beach somewhere."

"I hear you." He looked all around us, his cheeks darkening. "I'll never abandon Marcus and the Watchtower, but I'm tired of all of this. The hunting and the killing and the fighting. All of the goddamn pain."

"You know Rufus will give you a place in Ops the second you ask. You used to be a hacker for fuck's sake. You're the biggest geek we've got in this place."

"I know." He studied me, so serious in that moment. "What about you? What would you do if you didn't have to fight anymore?"

The million dollar question.

"You know what?" I said with a conviction that came from deep down where hope still flickered. "You and me, pal? We're both going to find out one day."

"Good answer, Evy. Now go take a shower. You reek."

I flipped him off, then headed for the apartment. The boys were there, watching a movie on the television, and they didn't make a single comment while I rummaged for clean clothes, and then disappeared into the bathroom.

A hot shower was pure heaven and fiery agony as the spray lifted drying goblin blood out of dozens of small cuts and gashes, many of them already beginning to heal. I'd be itchy as hell in about thirty minutes. My reflection still startled me, as it had when I first came back to life. Seven months ago, it was because I'd gone from skinny blonde with a page-cut to busty brunette with thick, long hair. Last week I'd chopped it all off and dyed it to go briefly under the radar.

The girl staring back at me from the mirror looked as exhausted as I felt inside. Exhausted of all of this. Exhausted of all the things Milo mentioned, and more. Mostly I wanted to be on that tropical beach with Wyatt, enjoying the rest of our lives in peace—except that wouldn't happen until this war with the Fey was over. Neither one of us could abandon the fight this close to the end.

Brevin's meeting with the Clan Elders and two vampire delegates would decide which way the winds of war would blow—and if we non-Fey had a chance in hell of winning.

CHAPTER FOUR

19:45

While our first meeting with Brevin had been as clandestine as possible, the main corridor was teaming with Watchtower members who weren't out on patrol, all eager for the first scraps of information about today's big show. Every single Therian Clan Elder was in attendance, some of them good friends and some tentative allies. Astrid and Marcus's cousin Riley Dane was the Felia Elder, and he looked so much like them they could have been siblings.

The War Room was full of Elders and their personal guards, as well as the top people in the Watchtower: Astrid, Marcus, Kismet, Rufus, Kyle, and Wyatt. I was there because I had war experience. Same reason my fellow humans Carly Hall, Paul Ryan and Seth Nevada were invited.

The vampires had sent Eulan and a woman I didn't know named Omal. I'd met Eulan a few times in the past, but I didn't get a chance to speak with him before the meeting. I wanted to know how Isleen was fairing now that she'd received the cure for a near-fatal virus that had infected many of our vampire allies at the Watchtower. Isleen and I had a long, sordid history, but at the end of the day, I was almost willing to call her a friend.

I was glad she wasn't dead, so that said something.

Our guests of honor sat around the entire perimeter of the conference table. Astrid and Kismet stood together at the head, waiting for the speaker of the hour to enter. Phineas had named himself Brevin's personal bodyguard, and he'd been with the elf almost non-stop since their arrival at the Watchtower, giving me precious little time to chat with my best friend.

I'd missed him while he was gone, and I still missed him while he was back.

The sudden silence in the room was as good as a bullhorn announcement. Phineas and Brevin stood in the archway that separated the War Room from the rest of Ops. Maybe he wanted to add a little drama to the proceedings, or maybe he wanted to remind the other Elders that he was one of the last of his kind of bi-shifting Therians, because Phin stood there shirtless, his large feathered wings arched high and to the side, a rainbow of browns and tans.

The first time I met Phin, he'd landed on the roof of a parked car, wings spread, like an angel fallen to earth. He was just as stunning today as he'd been all those months ago, a protector and a predator to his very core.

My attention shifted to the faces of the Elders around the table. Their expressions were fairly identical—skepticism mixed with alarm. Elves were extremely powerful magic users, living and breathing the power of the Break, more connected to it than any other Fey. Everyone here knew what Tovin had tried to do.

Just wait until they hear Brevin's plan for beating Amalie.

I'd had two days to wrap my head around the idea, and it still didn't sit right.

Phin led Brevin to the head of the table and stood next to Kismet. Brevin climbed onto the only vacant chair at the table, giving him more height and allow him a better view of the faces in attendance. Trepidation and curiosity thickened the air, tension pulling everything taut. No one spoke as Brevin took in his audience.

"Thank you for taking the time to hear me out on this grave matter before us," Brevin said, his voice clear and strong. "We disparate species stand at a crossroads unlike anything we have ever faced. A crossroads that could end in not only the destruction of the human race that we allowed millennia ago to rule this planet, but also of our own peoples. Therians. Vampires. Elves. Gargoyles. Goblins. So many others who aren't here today, but who might be gone tomorrow, if Amalie, Queen of Sprites, has her will be done.

"As many here are aware, all magic and beings tied to magic, are spun from the power of the Break. The name is very apropos, in that First Break is a rift in the fabric between two worlds. This world and the place where magic originated. While this universe was still in its infancy, we all lived on the other side of the Break. Until we discovered the rift to this world and a war began over closing the rift. We elves opposed, so we were banished to this slowly developing place as punishment. Your world was so young and untested, and we found ourselves enjoying the company of the strange creatures oozing out of your oceans and beginning to crawl on land.

"Others, of course, noticed the possibilities here, and they began to cross over. Our interference in the natural course of evolution brought about the creatures who would one day become the Therian Clans."

I glanced at Phineas, because yeah, that was news. Looked like news to him, too, if his arched eyebrows were any indication.

"When mankind first began to walk upright, the Tainted took notice. They were attracted to the weakness in your minds, and they came to wreak havoc. To influence and dominate humankind and make them their slaves. The Fey Council, of course, opposed this. Humankind was slowly overtaking the world, coming into their own sense of power, as was their right. All of this happened over many millennia to you, but for the Fey it lasted such a short time."

We'd been told more than once that the Fey experienced time differently. What lasted a week for us might be only a minute for a sprite or an elf. It gave us an advantage in terms of preparation and improvising.

"Elves and Fey banded together to hunt and banish the Tainted back across the Break to our old world. It took many thousands of years, and the last was sent over in your Middle Ages, but not before causing the Black Death."

Something the history books never told us: Black Death initiated by grumpy demons.

"For many centuries afterward there was peace. My people once held the highest position of power among us, higher even than the Fey. We flourished, as did the species under our protection, including humankind. Until the sprites got greedy. They disagreed with our decision to disappear from the eyes of the world. Amalie turned the other Fey against us, and we were hunted. Only three of elves remain alive, and our days are dwindling. Soon the last of the elves will walk this world, and then be gone. And if that is to be our fate, I will die knowing the rightful inheritors of this world still own it, and that the Fey have not destroyed humankind and all who live among them."

"Why did elves choose to disappear from the world?" Eulan asked.

Leave it to a vampire to want a history lesson. Not that I wasn't curious. Last week we'd been given an ancient scroll that supposedly told the history of the elves, but it was written in a forgotten form of Aramaic, so our attempts to decipher it led us nowhere. We'd already gotten a head-full of information from Brevin, and I was actually kind of enjoying the lecture.

"The various mythologies of humankind are all influenced by the presence of the Fair Folk in the wider world. Name your country or culture, and we are there. We were Zeus and Coyote and Hachiman and Vishnu. But humankind was not meant to worship at the feet of imaginary gods. You had your own destinies to create, and so the decision was made to step aside. We helped create the stories still spun today in order to hide the truth of our being, and it has worked. Only a scant few know of the true existence of the nonhumans who walk this world."

Brevin's gaze traveled around the room, pausing on each human in attendance. I refused to meet his eyes when he zeroed in on me.

"So you stepped aside," Astrid said. "Amalie didn't like it, and now she's preparing to do what? Start some kind of magical war in order to eradicate mankind?"

"I have no illusions that she will stop with humankind," Brevin said. "All who oppose her, and even some who ally with her, may face extinction. Or enslavement, as was once the case with the vampires."

That got my attention. I perked up, sharing a confused look with Wyatt. Most of the Therians seemed just as surprised by the comment. Only Eulan and Omal were nonreactive.

"The Fey enslaved the vampires?" Astrid asked Brevin as much as the pair of Bloods in attendance.

"They were Fey themselves once, long before humankind learned to walk upright," Brevin said.

"Holy shitballs," Milo said in my ear, and it took all of my personal self-control not to jump when he hollered.

Had I forgotten to mention that I went into the meeting on a live cell phone call to Milo, with a Bluetooth in my ear? He'd wanted to listen in, and no one had actually told me that it was forbidden.

No shit, holy shitballs.

Apparently this was a bedtime story told to baby vampires, because Eulan and Omal merely nodded along.

"They were the lowest of the Fey," Brevin said. "They had very little power, their ties to the Break far too weak to be any real use to us other than as servants. We kept them docile by creating their addiction to the blood of mammals less intelligent than they. Little did we know those idiot mammals would become the ancestors of humankind and that their blood lust would never fade."

No, it didn't fade, it became a goddamn dependence that we were still paying for, thank you very much.

"Idiot mammals," Carly murmured. "Gee, thanks."

I held back a derisive snort.

"When did you free them?" Elder Dane asked, the first elder to speak up.

"When we disappeared from the world," Brevin replied. "We had no use for them any longer, so we allowed them to create their own paths."

Paths that turned humans into snack foods. Fantastic.

"While I am certain the ill-informed appreciate the history lesson," Omal said—and I swear that sounded like an insult to everyone in the room—"we are here to listen to your suggestion on how to stop Amalie and her followers."

"You are correct," Brevin said. "Months ago, my brother Tovin sought to bring one of the Tainted across the Break and install it in the body of a human male. He assumed that by controlling the free will of the male, he would also control the Tainted. He was wrong."

Yeah, no shit.

Next to me, Wyatt was so tense I feared he might spontaneously sprain something. We'd both heard this before, at our first meeting with Tovin, but that didn't make hearing it again any less stressful. Or crazy.

"Tovin was the youngest of we four, and also the most impulsive. His intentions were good, however his logic was flawed in two places."

"Only two?" Marcus said softly.

Brevin ignored him. "First, Tovin chose to use a human male. Human bodies are too fragile to successfully hold or control the power of a Tainted. Had Tovin been successful in bringing the Tainted across, the chosen male would have been torn apart within hours."

Several sets of eyeballs glanced toward Wyatt, who was still laser-focused on the elf.

"Tovin's second error was in attempting to control the free will of the chosen vessel. In order for the vessel to successfully coexist with the Tainted, they must do so of *their* own free will. It is a path they must choose. Only then will the partnership work, and only then will we have warriors strong enough to defeat the Fey."

"In summation," Elder Dane said, "you want Therians to voluntary house a demon in order to wage this war?"

"Yes."

Milo was panting in my ear a little bit, probably freaking out over the enormity of what was happening. And it was pretty fucking huge.

"What happens to the volunteer?" Elder Rojay of Cania asked. "Assuming we win this war, can the Tainted be sent back? Will the volunteer be as they once were?"

Brevin shook his head. "I do not know. Such a thing as this has never before been attempted. The Tainted may consume them by the end. The Tainted may be banished back across the Break, leaving the volunteer as they are now. I simply do not know."

The not knowing is what broke my heart. My friends could volunteer to take part in what was basically a kamikaze mission—house a demon, fight a war, possibly die for it.

"You're asking for a lot of trust," Astrid said. "Trust that the Tainted can be controlled, and trust that this will be enough to stop Amalie."

"I am offering a suggestion," Brevin replied. "If you have another plan to stop the Fey, I will not be offended if you do not accept the help of the elves. I will return to my path and leave you to your choices."

"How many volunteers are you talking about?" Elder Rojay asked.

"Three. I can only summon one Tainted. My two living brothers will join us and help, if this is your wish."

A lot of murmurs went up around the table as the various Elders began speaking to each other. I actively hated this plan, but like I had during the initial meeting three days ago, I believed it was our *best* plan. In many ways, it was our only plan. Once Amalie set her mind to it, she could do a lot of damage very quickly. The only thing we had going for us was Amalie's age. Since sprites lived to be thousands of years old, two weeks for a human was mere seconds for her.

We had time on our side, but even that would run out eventually. It always did.

"I know this is a huge decision," Astrid said, addressing the entire room. "But I've been considering this information for the last three days, and I do believe it's our best option. I know that for many of you, the idea of a war with the Fey is laughable. You may assume it won't happen in your lifetime, and perhaps that's true. But what about the next generation of Therians? Do we foist this responsibility upon them, or do we stand up now and take a proactive stance against an attack we know will happen. If not today, maybe six months from now. Or sixty years from now. It doesn't matter. We are standing on the brink of history, and I'm not willing back down."

Astrid turned to face Brevin, her face set and stony. "I volunteer to house one of the Tainted."

"What?"

I turned off the Bluetooth. I didn't need Milo in my ear, and he could hear all about it later.

"No," Marcus said. He turned his sister to face him. "You lead this initiative, Astrid. You're needed here, captaining your soldiers. Soldiers who will need you to lead them into this upcoming war."

Shit. I saw it coming in the subtle way Marcus's lips went flat.

He looked at Brevin and said, "I volunteer in my sister's place. No matter the outcome, I will fight for my people's future."

Astrid looked pained, but didn't argue.

No one else spoke up, but many of the Elders were regarding Marcus with open respect.

"This is not a decision to be taken lightly," Brevin said. "However, it is not one that can be taken at leisure. The sooner we begin, the sooner it will end. If more volunteer, then I will summon my kin. And that is all I have to say."

The room erupted in loud conversation, mostly from the Elders. I held back by the wall, glaring silently at Marcus, furious at him for volunteering. The only thing keeping me from yelling at him right then was that he was surrounded by other people. Thank fuck I'd turned off the call to Milo before Marcus volunteered himself. Milo needed Marcus, and the stupid cat had gone and decided to house a fucking demon.

My phone buzzed in my pocket. I ignored the call.

Wyatt stuck close, whispering the occasional comment that he heard with his super ears. A lot of hesitation from the Equi and Prosi, while the Cania, Ursia and Felia were all in. Debates about acceptable risks and why on earth they should trust Brevin. It went on and on for about an hour, with Milo calling my cell on and off. I felt bad for ignoring him, but nothing had actually been decided yet. Finally I texted him. **Still debating. Will let you know when I know.**

Kismet and Rufus joined us on our side of the room.

"How do you think it's going?" Kismet asked. She had scratches all over her face and neck, many of them red and angry.

"Difficult to tell," Wyatt replied. "The majority are leaning toward trusting Brevin. The big question seems to be the matter of volunteers. The more Clan members the Elders ask, the more know what we're planning."

"And the more people who know a secret, the bigger chance it will get leaked to the wrong person."

"Exactly."

"I'm surprised Marcus volunteered." She sounded as happy about it as I was.

"I'm not." Wyatt rolled his shoulders. "He's a warrior. He knows what's at stake."

"Damn," I said. "Wyatt, I think that's the nicest thing you've ever said about Marcus."

Wyatt raised an eyebrow in response.

I met Kismet's green eyes and knew she was thinking the same as me: Milo. How on earth would he react to knowing Marcus could go into a potentially fatal battle? Sure, any of us could die on any given day, during any mission, but this was practically committing suicide. No one could guarantee that the volunteers would survive hosting a demon, must less using one to fight Amalie.

"I volunteer!"

Ice water trickled down my spine at the too familiar voice shouting to be heard. The din instantly went silent, heads turning to find the source. I pinned him with a hard stare and from across the room, he met my eyes.

"I volunteer as the second host," Phineas said. He tore his gaze from mine and looked at Marcus. "I will fight beside you in this battle."

Marcus nodded.

"The Ursia Clan stands beside you both," their Elder said. I couldn't remember his name, but he had the multi-hued hair color familiar to his Clan.

Elder Dane was standing next to him. "As do the Felia."

"Cania as well," Elder Rojay said.

In the end nine out of the twelve Clans agreed to support the Watchtower and Brevin's plan. Considering the critters that chose to sit this one out—raccoons, bush-babies, and komodo dragons—we were in good shape in terms of warriors. Plus three of the nine were bi-shifters like Phineas. The vampires agreed to assist as able, since a lot of their people were still recovering.

Not too shabby a lineup for a bunch of species that used to hate each other.

The meeting was adjourned so that a third volunteer could be found. Phineas disappeared with Brevin before I could corner him.

Marcus wasn't so lucky. "Are you insane?" I snapped.

His copper eyes flashed with anger and frustration. "I wasn't going to let Astrid volunteer. The Watchtower needs her here."

"So you volunteered to be a demon-sitter in her place?"

"I didn't exactly think it through. All I knew in that moment was my sister, this organization's leader, had put herself in unnecessary danger. So I fixed it."

I crossed my arms. "That what you're going to tell Milo."

Marcus's anger melted away, and he almost looked sad. "I don't know. He's all I've been able to think about since I said yes." He glanced past me, probably at Wyatt, who was always nearby lately. "He'll understand."

"Part of him will. The Hunter in him understands duty and sacrifice. The man who looks at you like you're the most valuable thing on the planet? It'll break his heart. And you won't be around for me to murder in his defense."

"The last thing I ever want to do is hurt Milo. He's been hurt enough."

"Yeah, he has." I'd seen the old scars on his back, probably from beatings as a child. We all had scars of some kind, visible or not. I glanced around the nearly empty conference room. Astrid and Eulan were speaking quietly in one corner. Wyatt stood nearby listening to me and Marcus.

"Perhaps it's better this way," Marcus said.

"Excuse me? Better for who?"

"Milo is young. He has decades of life ahead of him. I'm already at the halfway point of my life, Evangeline. I have maybe ten more years, and at the end I'll be more like his grandfather than his lover. He deserves better than that."

Wow. Marcus's words stunned me into silence, as truthful as they were…well, romantic. I had no idea the big were-cat had it in him. "Milo's young, but he knows what you are. And anyone who's ever been a Hunter knows that tomorrow isn't promised to anyone. Especially those of us who fight."

"Hey, guys." Milo's voice startled us both. He leaned on his walker in the doorway that led out into Ops. "Everyone's saying that we're going along with Brevin's plan. That true?"

"Yes, that's true," Marcus replied. The immediate affection in his eyes made me hate him a little bit less. "Can we speak? In private."

"That's my cue to leave," I said.

Wyatt trailed me through Ops and out into the main corridor. Most of the Elders had been escorted to their cars, but a lot of the Watchtower crew still loitered, chatting in clumps spread up and down the hall. I wanted to talk to Phineas, but he wasn't anywhere in sight. I probably could have asked Wyatt to track him down by scent, except that always felt creepy. I hated it when Therians sniffed me out.

"Who do you think the third volunteer will be?" Wyatt asked.

"Difficult to say." I let him wrap his arms around my middle. Reclining against his chest and allowing him to hold me was so natural now. Even in front of others. "I hope it's a stranger from one of the Clans and not someone else I care about."

"No matter who it is, someone will care about them."

"I know. Fuck, I don't want Phin to do this." My throat squeezed tight at the idea of him not being there anymore. And not just gone off to try and find others of his kind, but gone as in dead. Destroyed by some evil magical entity from the inside out. Just…no.

"Phin comes from one of the oldest, strongest Therian Clans. If anyone can survive this, it's him."

"Are you saying that to make me feel better?"

"No." He turned me in his arms, truth shining from his silver flecked eyes. "I say it because I believe it, and I need you to believe it, too."

I didn't totally believe it, but I believed in Wyatt. That had to be enough for now.

"Truman!" Paul was running toward us from the south end of the mall, face red from the discomfort of his still healing shoulder wounds from last week. "Need you in the cafeteria, ASAP."

Wyatt took off running, too damned fast for me to keep up, and he was turning into the cafeteria before I was halfway there. The room was mostly empty, and a handful of tables in the rear were overturned. Mark and Peter stood against the wall, huddling together like something had frightened them. Several people stood around, looking down at a central point.

Said central point being Wyatt and John. The latter was on his butt, arms wrapped around his knees, head down, rocking back and forth. Wyatt was kneeling in front of him, whispering something I couldn't hear. Paul and Alejandro loitered nearby. The other three watching were all Therians, somewhat new to the Watchtower, but one had the copper eyes of a Felia.

"What the fuck happened?" I asked.

The Felia flinched at my tone, and yeah, I was developing a Mom Voice. The Therians stayed silent, so I switched my glare to Paul and Alejandro.

"I just got here from the meeting and saw something going down," Paul said. "As soon as I saw the boys were involved, I got Truman."

It was bizarre to hear Paul refer to a trio of sixteen year-olds as "boys" when he was only a day past nineteen himself.

"Alejandro?" I said.

"I was eating by myself," he said. "I wasn't involved, I swear."

Alejandro was one of our newest human recruits to the Watchtower. Newest meaning only a week or so. He'd been trained as a Hunter, and then basically orphaned when our training camp was destroyed. He'd tracked me down on the streets and kind of begged for work. So far he'd proven himself honest, capable, and loyal—if a little too earnest.

"They started teasing us," Mark said. His face was flushed, eyes bright. I wasn't used to seeing the pups angry. "All three of them. They called us mongrels, said we should have been put down like our brothers."

That got a seriously dangerous growl from Wyatt that made all three Therians take a full step backward.

"What happened to John?" I asked.

"The cat." Mark pointed at the Felia, his expression thunderous. "He asked John what it was like to submit to Vale as his captive, and John lost it."

My own temper was starting to peak at dangerous levels. John had been kidnapped, beaten, and traumatized only a few days ago. Even with their faster healing rate, the kid still had a lot of mental shit to work through. PTSD didn't bypass Therians.

The fucktwat Felia was on his back, blood spurting from his nose before I felt the impact shock through my knuckles and up my arm. I glared down at him, breathing hard from adrenaline, seriously itching to kick the fucker while he was down. "How *dare* you?"

"Evangeline, stop." John's broken voice penetrated my fog of anger.

I turned. He looked up at me, eyes wide and fearful, skin terribly pale. "Are you okay?"

"No. But please, no more violence because of me. There's been too much."

I squatted next to him, which gave me a good view of just how furious Wyatt was—full silver eyes, check. Constant guttural growl, check. I squeezed John's shoulder, pleased he didn't shrink from my touch. "You're Wyatt's family, John, which makes you my family. And I don't let asswipes like that hurt my family."

"He didn't hurt me. He didn't even touch me."

"You can hurt with words, too." I looked at Mark and Peter. "You boys aren't in any trouble. You either, John. But you three." I leveled a deadly glare on the trio of cowering Therians. "You can report straight to Astrid about why your nose is broken. And if I hear anything different than the truth from her, I'll give you a broken jaw to go with it."

All three scampered off, and it might have been funny if I wasn't still so pissed.

"They'll never accept us," Peter said. "Will they?"

"They isn't a person," I replied. "Felia and Lupa are enemies to their core. It's instinctive for Felia to lash out, but they're also in enough control of their beast to keep that instinct in check. There is no excuse for how you were treated."

"I think they're scared of us too," John said. "We're more dangerous to humans than any other Therian."

"Maybe, but no Therian poses the same threat level to humans as the vampires, and they still exist freely."

"You three deserve a safe life," Wyatt said. His voice was thick and growly, as if he was still struggling to keep his beast under control. "I promised it to you when you agreed to live here under my protection, and I'm promising it again."

"Thank you." John glanced up at his brothers, who both nodded their agreement.

My hand twinged as I stood. I'd managed to split a knuckle when I punched that cat in the nose. Add it to the long list of healing wounds. I wouldn't have minded taking another swing at the bastard, and that kind of surprised me.

I don't know when it happened, but I cared about those Lupa pups.

God help anyone who tried to hurt them again.

CHAPTER FIVE

18:30

Instead of taking my bad mood out on Wyatt or anyone else, I helped him get the pups back to our apartment, and then I hit the gym. More specifically, I hit one of the heavy bags in the gym. A lot. For a long time. Until my arms felt like jelly and I'd worked up a pretty gross sweat.

I took off my gloves and threw them hard at the far wall. They didn't give me the satisfying thud I wanted. I landed a good roundhouse kick on the bag, then dropped three more. It wasn't enough. The anger was still there, simmering beneath the surface like molten lava, waiting for the right crack to be released.

"I imagine you're picturing my face on that bag." Phineas's voice drifted over, at once a calming balm and a crack on an already shaky surface.

"Not just yours." I turned, careful not to glare. He stood near the gym's entrance, arms loose by his sides.

"I'm pissed at a lot of people right now, including myself."

"Why are you angry at yourself?"

"Because I can't do anything to help this time." The unexpectedly honest reply shattered my resistance, and that furious lava boiled up and out. I punched the bag with my bare knuckles, hard enough to split more skin.

Arms like steel bands wrapped around my waist and hauled me back, still swinging, trying to exorcise the fear and helplessness that were being masked as rage. Phineas held me until I stopped struggling and sagged against his chest.

"I can't fucking do anything," I said. "I can't volunteer to host one of the Tainted, because it would tear me apart, Gifted or not. You know me, Phin. I'm a soldier. I fight, I don't sit by and watch others fight for me."

"You are a born warrior, Evangeline, as am I."

"Is that why you volunteered?"

"Partly. My people were once the strongest, fiercest of all Therian warriors. Fighting is in our blood."

"I get that. But you could die."

"I know." He turned me around, hands solid weights on my shoulders. "We could both die at any moment. But I'm also doing this for Aurora and Ava. I want to give them a safe world to live their lives, even if it means sacrificing my own."

"Aurora wouldn't want you to."

"I know. In a way, I'm glad she's disappeared. Perhaps she'll never learn how close to Armageddon we've come."

"Meanwhile, the rest of us are stuck here staring Armageddon up the ass and pretending we aren't all scared to death of what it's going to shit out."

"I so missed your colorful phrasing while I was away." Phineas's smile was tinged with sadness. "Bi-shifters are the strongest candidates as Tainted hosts. I have no wife or children to risk leaving behind."

"No, just a bunch of friends who love your self-sacrificing ass."

"I love you, as well. You are a cherished friend."

"Ditto. So maybe do your best not to be overtaken or destroyed or whatever by this demon you're going to host."

"I'll do my best." His hands fell to his sides. "I must admit, I was surprised when Marcus volunteered to do it in place of his sister."

"I'm not. The idiot is so noble he bleeds it."

"I imagine his conversation with Milo will be a difficult one."

"Yeah, that's going to go over like a brick to the head." I wanted to check on Milo, but he might not be finished strangling Marcus yet. I'd never been close enough to Marcus or Astrid to pose the question, but there wasn't much I was afraid to say to Phin's face. "Are there very many gay Therians?"

"Few that I'm aware of, but homosexual urges exist in most species on this planet. For us, however, short life spans require frequent reproduction. Our Clans are already quite small compared to other species. Most would be classified as close to extinction if we were known to the general public. Marcus made a brave choice in his decision not to marry and to be open about his feelings for another male."

"A very human male."

Phineas smiled, showing off wickedly white teeth. "We cannot control who our heart chooses."

Something in the soft inflection of his voice made me wonder how personal that statement was. "Phineas el Chimal, are you seeing someone?"

"Seeing someone?" He blinked at me. "I'm seeing you."

"No, not literally, you dork. Are you dating someone? Interested in? Have a crush on?" I needed good gossip. Happy news.

His lips twitched. "Perhaps."

"Really? Who?"

"No. She threatened to gouge my eyes out with a dull spoon if I told anyone, and I risk her wrath by telling you this much."

I planted both hands on my hips. "That's mean. If I guess right, will you tell me?"

"No."

"Spoil sport. I could always ask Wyatt to smell you."

"Pardon me?"

Phin's affronted look made me laugh. "Come on, Therians are always sniffing everybody, and if one more person says I smell like Wyatt, I am going to break their face."

For a moment, Phineas seemed seriously worried I'd sic Wyatt on him, so I backed off.

"Okay, fine, I won't try to find out who you're seeing," I said. "I'm sure she'll tear a strip off your hide later for volunteering."

"Yes, I was hoping to avoid that conversation for as long as possible. Your wrath, while powerful, is far less devastating."

Sounds as if he really likes whoever she is.

A tiny part of me was jealous of this mystery lover, but most of me was happy for Phineas. He deserved someone special in his life for however much time he had. "Well, if you need a bodyguard, let me know."

"I doubt it will come to that, but I appreciate the offer." He clasped one of my hands with his. "I know how difficult this will be for you, watching those you care about sacrifice for you when you're used to being the one sacrificing herself for others."

I held tight, grateful for his comforting touch. "I used to think I wanted to die fighting, defending my friends or innocent lives. I used to want to go out in a blaze of bloody glory and take my enemies down with me."

"And now?"

"I want a beach. I want quiet. I want someone to bring me fruity drinks with umbrellas in them. And I want to be there with Wyatt, for the rest of our lives."

"If I've learned anything about you, Evangeline Stone, it's that when you set your mind on something, you get it. Hold on tightly to that dream until it comes true."

"Thank you."

A soft growl from my right announced Wyatt's arrival before I spotted him glaring at us from the gym's entrance. Phineas, in an interesting display of dominance, lifted my hand and kissed my knuckles before releasing me.

"We'll speak again soon," he said.

"Definitely."

Phineas had to circle around Wyatt to leave the gym. Wyatt's glare softened into a grimace as he walked to me. "Sorry."

"Sorry for what? Growling at Phin?"

"Well, not exactly. He was touching you."

"Platonically, you jealous idiot."

"I'm sorry for growling because of the conversation you were probably having. Phineas is your friend, and he's chosen a dangerous assignment."

"Yeah, well, apparently someone else is going to be giving him hell for that later." I filled him in on Phineas's avoidance of the dating topic. "I am insanely curious now. Phin has always been so…I don't know. I mean, I know he had a wife and child once, but he's so much about work and being a warrior and stuff."

"And you're not?"

"Yeah, well I have you, don't I?" I planted a kiss on his mouth. "What have you been up to?"

"Discussing engagement tactics with Astrid. According to Brevin, the magic necessary to bring the Tainted across the Break will be enough to get Amalie's undivided attention, no matter where she is in the world. So when this goes down, the rest of us have to be ready."

"Oh joy. How the hell do you fight sprites and sylphs?"

"Amalie's human avatar is dead, but she's apparently powerful enough to commandeer another one as long as their mind is weak or distracted enough. So we could end up facing an army of sprites in human bodies."

I groaned. Not good. Sprites are tiny things, maybe four feet tall, with colorful hair and jewel-encrusted skin. Not physically powerful, but they made up for it with magic. Amalie and her bodyguard Jaron used to make contact by telepathically taking over the minds of human beings and using their bodies for a while. The human apparently remembered nothing about it, but some of them went a little crazy due to all of the lost time.

The very last thing we needed was to try and battle magically-controlled humans. We didn't kill humans. Not on purpose. "But aren't the Fey supposed to be pacifists? Would they do that?"

"I don't honestly know, Evy. Amalie said so herself in First Break, but it could have been a total lie. She's deceived us before."

"True. What about her other followers? Gnomes, fairies, pixies? Are there dwarves? Tell me there aren't dwarves."

"Gnomes are healers. They won't engage, and Horzt even said they're going north, away from the city. According to Brevin—and I'm taking his word because I've never seen a pixie before—are kind of like butterflies with razor teeth and venom. Too many bites can leave a person paralyzed."

"Peter Pan would not be pleased."

Wyatt snorted.

"So can't we create some kind of magical, anti-fairy bug spray or something?" I asked.

"Astrid is looking into it."

"Oh. Really?" Here I thought I was being funny. "Okay then."

"And, unfortunately, yes, dwarves do exist, and they're apparently a close cousin race to goblins."

"You have got to be shitting me."

Wyatt shook his head. "They were described as hair-covered goblins, similar in size, who walk much like a gorilla. They're able to go on two feet, but move more quickly on all fours. The same long, sharp claws, but they lack the teeth."

"Dwarves are hairy goblins." I rolled my eyes. "My second life is now complete."

"Wouldn't Tolkien be surprised?"

"About my life?"

That got a genuine smile out of him. "About what dwarves really look like. But I suppose legend was correct about their love of caves. Apparently dwarves spend most of their lives underground, digging for precious metals and diamonds."

"Seriously?"

"I'm repeating what I was told. Brevin says dwarves have a serious weakness for diamonds. Aside from being photophobic, diamonds will stop them in their tracks, and they are totally mesmerized by the glittering."

"Oh good, I've always wanted to go into battle wearing a diamond tiara." I let go of my sarcasm long enough to catch what else he said. "Wait, photophobic?"

"Even more than vampires. Because they spend most of their lives underground, their skin is incredibly sensitive to light, and even with their eyes shut, sunlight blinds them into immobility."

"So our best chance of winning is if we start this pissing match first thing in the morning on a sunny day."

"Correct."

"Then let's hope no one tries to start shit today. It's supposed to rain into the evening."

The thought did not fill me with joy. Nor did the realization that the magic memory potion Astrid had sent me to fetch was probably still in the car, waiting to be used on them. As my anger and adrenaline waned, an unwanted flash of anxiety jolted through me. The Frosts needed to be dealt with, but I still hesitated in using magic on them. Something could very easily go terribly wrong.

Aches in my fingers stole me back to the situation at hand. I'd beaten the hell out of a bag without gloves, not long after breaking that asshat Therian's nose, and I was feeling it. Wyatt slipped an arm around my shoulders, and I leaned into him.

"You know something?" he asked quietly.

"What?"

"I'd love to see you go into battle wearing a diamond tiara."

I laughed, then pinched his ass, and for a brief moment, everything was okay.

Astrid wasn't happy about me punching that Felia, but she also didn't pitch much of a fit. Wyatt and I grabbed a quick lunch, then returned to the apartment to be with the boys for a while. We didn't have anything to do until orders were given, or we were sent on patrol, and I wasn't about to remind Astrid of the memory potion, so we watched TV.

It was really weird, but also really fucking nice as a change of pace.

In the middle of the afternoon, our phones both dinged with a message from Ops. An Equi named Boone had volunteered to be the third host. I'd met him a handful of times in passing. He was young, only five years old, and a Clydesdale-shifter so the guy was huge in both forms. Three volunteers meant Brevin was contacting his kin, so we were expecting two more elves among us by the end of the day.

I wasn't sure if that was good news or the start of the end of times.

No more goblins had been spotted at the junkyard, so with help from the owners, the sewer access was permanently sealed shut and the VW bus cleaned up. Ops was still working on matching the remains to missing persons reports, but chances were good that the victims had been homeless and no one was missing them.

A little after three p.m., whatever program we were mindlessly watching on TV flashed to a news report.

"We apologize for this interruption of your regular programming," an old guy with white hair said, hands clutching sheets of paper. His co-anchor was a blond lady who looked a little shell-shocked. *"We have just received word that the Coliseum in Rome has crumbled to the ground."*

I sat up straighter.

"The hell?" Wyatt said.

"Reports state that the ground near the Coliseum began to shake, and large parts of the structure began falling away and shattering. Hundreds of tourists are currently trapped inside of the debris."

The screen shifted to a shaky video that was obviously taken from someone's cell phone, showing a giant chunk of stone hitting the pavement and cracking.

"No other earthquakes have been reported in other parts of the city, and it is unknown exactly what caused the thousands of years old structure to collapse. Emergency crews are already on the scene. Tune in to our regularly scheduled newscast at four for further updates."

The screen flashed to the news logo, then returned to the program.

The pups looked up at us. I met Wyatt's gaze. "Trolls?"

He nodded. "You boys stay here."

Wyatt was on the phone with Astrid before we left the apartment. A general alert went out to quad leaders to meet in the War Room. By the time everyone arrived, including Phineas and Brevin, more reports of destruction had come over. The Karnak Temple in Egypt, the Mogao Caves in China, and the Western Wall in

Jerusalem had all been toppled by unexpected, unexplainable earthquakes.

Religious symbols for different religions, all across the world.

"Amalie is striking first blood," Phineas said.

"But how—?" Marcus started.

"Trolls," I said. "She's using the trolls still loyal to her."

It hurt knowing a former ally of mine, a bridge troll named Smedge, could have been one of the trolls destroying ancient landmarks. He'd saved my life once, and then helped a gnome reach out and provide us with a cure for the infected vampires. I hadn't had direct contact with him in weeks, though, and most trolls were loyal to the Fey.

"If she's using trolls to attack from below, then we can't wait," Astrid said. To Brevin she said, "When your kin arrive, how long do you need to prepare for this ritual?"

"Several hours, at least," Brevin said. "Sunrise is the ideal hour, for it is when magic is at its strongest. The birth of the new day. We will also require access to First Break."

First Break was the place where magic originated from, and there were two points of access that I knew about. The first was the underground city where Amalie and her Fair Ones once resided beneath the Anjean River. Instinct told me they no longer lived there, especially since Wyatt and I knew about a tunnel that opened up deep in Mercy's Lot.

The second point of access wasn't much to look at. A round hole in the ground that looked like shiny black water, deep in an underground cave close to the Fey city. After Tovin tried to pull a Tainted over, we'd bulldozed the building hiding the Break and slathered the ground with asphalt so no one could get down there.

Point number two would be easier to get to, and had Tovin seemed okay with using it, as opposed to the magic pool in Amalie's backyard.

"That's going to take some time," Kismet said. "We buried that place earlier this year."

Brevin fixed her with a bland look. "Then I suggest someone un-buries it."

"Already on it," Rufus said. A lot of heads turned his way, including mine. He shrugged. "Clearly Astrid and I were the only ones thinking ahead that far?"

The idea of returning to the location of Wyatt's death sent a funny chill through my chest. For a brief time, I'd lost him, and I never wanted to feel that spearing pain again.

"You'll have access by midnight tonight," Rufus told Brevin.

"Excellent."

"So what do the rest of us get to do in the meantime?" I asked.

Brevin's bland expression was starting to irritate me. "Prepare yourselves for the final battle against the Fey. I have no doubt that once we begin the process of freeing the Tainted, Amalie will take notice and send her people to stop us. We will be at war."

At war. Humans, vampires, and shifters against sprites, fairies and dwarves. Humanoids versus magical beings.

Fucking fantastic.

CHAPTER SIX

13:30

Milo wasn't at dinner, and he wasn't with Marcus, because Marcus, Phineas, and Boone were meeting with the now-two elves currently haunting our hallways. With the excuse that the gimp needed to eat, I took a plate back to his room at the dorms and wasn't surprised to find him on his bed, earbuds in, listening to something on his phone.

I tapped the foot of the bed with my boot.

He glared at me but didn't otherwise move.

"I brought you food." Obviously, since I had a plate with a hamburger and bag of chips in one hand and bottle of water in the other.

He closed his eyes.

Okay, we're doing it the hard way.

I put the food down on his side table, then climbed onto the bed to sit cross-legged by his left hip. He opened his eyes again, then tugged out the earbuds.

"I'm not in the mood, Evy."

"I bet you aren't." I hated the anger and grief in his eyes. "No one is."

"Yeah, well, it's not your boyfriend who's about to house a demon, is it?"

"No, but my best friend is—wait, boyfriend?"

He sat up with a bit of a struggle, resisting my help with an unexpected snarl. "I can do it, fuck." When he got himself settled again, he looked near tears. "It's not fair. Not after Felix and then Tybalt. I can't lose Marcus, too."

We'd both lost a lot of people we loved in a very short amount of time, and we'd both grieved a lot. But in the year and a half year since I'd known Milo, I had never seen him so emotionally vulnerable as in that moment. He'd buried two of his brothers, and now he was facing the loss of a man he cared for a great deal—maybe even loved.

I found myself in the odd position of being the one to offer hope. "We don't know that the Tainted will destroy them. Not even Brevin is certain of the outcome."

"Not knowing makes it worse. At least if we were sure, we could say goodbye and mean it, you know? I could start letting him go, instead of clinging so tightly it hurts."

I grabbed his hand, and he let me, squeezing back. In some ways, I wanted to know with certainty what would happen. Certainty meant saying goodbye to our loved ones properly. Even though uncertainty gave me hope for a good outcome, it also meant the opposite. I couldn't reconcile the idea that in roughly twelve hours, Phineas would be the physical host to a demon. All three men who volunteered were fighting for the good of every species, yes, but at a personal level, all three were fighting for the people they loved.

"Marcus volunteered in the heat of the moment to protect Astrid," I said. "But I know he's doing it to protect you, too. Anyone with eyes in their head can see how much you mean to him. He wants to give you a better world to live in."

"Without him."

"Maybe." Marcus's words about it being best this way, about his own mortality, flittered past but I didn't voice them. Milo wasn't thinking about ten years from now, when Marcus's lifespan would be at its end. Hunters didn't think that far ahead. We lived for the now, and right now, Milo was in so much pain.

I didn't know how to help him.

"There's still so much we haven't done." Milo's whispered words seemed more for himself than for me.

Didn't stop me from being nosy. "Like what?"

His cheeks pinked up, and he looked away.

Oh? Oh! Duh.

If I'd only had a few hours left to say goodbye to Wyatt, you'd better believe that making love was on the agenda. Milo had admitted to one unexpected kiss before the beating from Vale, and then the one I'd witnessed in the infirmary after the fight with Vale. I couldn't imagine

Milo had been in any shape to do physical stuff with Marcus since then. Milo's embarrassment also held a lot of longing, and I resisted the strange urge to hug him until he felt better.

Nothing was going to make him feel better except a safe, healthy Marcus back in his arms after this war was over.

"I want him so badly, but he treats me like I'm made of glass," Milo said after a moment of awkward silence. "And yeah, maybe it wouldn't be super gymnastical, but it would mean something. It would mean so much for it to be him."

That one hit me like a sledgehammer. "You're a virgin?"

Milo covered his face with a pillow, which said yes for him. It was both incredibly adorable and kind of sad, considering how many close shaves with death he'd had lately. Anyone with that much pain and life experience under their belt deserved a good fuck once in a while.

"Dude, I'm not laughing at you, I promise."

"Yes, you are." Muffled but audible.

"No, really." I yanked the pillow away.

He glared. "Look, I've fooled around and gotten off with guys, but it never felt…safe being that vulnerable."

"We are talking about fucking, right?"

The glare went up a notch. "Yes."

"Just checking." I folded my arms and had a moment of What Would Evy Do? "Want my advice?"

"I don't know."

"Tell him. Sit Marcus down and tell him you want to make love before he becomes a demon holder, and that you won't take no for an answer."

"He won't, will he?" Marcus's deep voice bounced around the small room.

Milo flushed bright red, and I swear he nearly covered himself with the pillow again.

Since Milo seemed to have trouble standing up for what he wanted in regards to the big were-cat, I stood up for him. Literally and figuratively. "He likes you a hell of a lot for some reason," I said. "So much so that he'll ignore some aches and pains in order to be with you, even if only for one night. He deserves at least that much, Marcus."

Marcus regarded me for a moment, his neutral expression never changing.

"Do me a favor," I continued. "Turn off your phones, lock the door, and then spend some time fucking each other's brains out. Give yourself something to come home for. Give Milo something to hope for."

That neutral look softened into a smile, and I gave a silent cheer. "If Astrid wonders where I am?" he asked.

"I'll tell her you're busy and are not to be disturbed unless the end of the world is nigh."

"The end of the world *is* nigh."

"We've got a few hours yet before dawn. Go with it, big guy."

I let myself out and shut the door behind me. I'd done my duty as Milo's best friend. Whatever else happened was between them.

An hour later I was busy helping Shelby and Kyle stockpile weapons into one of our vans when all of our phones alerted at once.

911. Goblins loose in Briar's Ridge Mall. All hands on deck.

"This can't be serious," Kyle said. "What the hell are goblins doing in the mall?"

"It's not early Christmas shopping," I retorted. "Shit."

Shelby climbed into the front seat, and I took shotgun. The van could comfortably fit six more bodies, but we squeezed in nine, including Boone and Phineas, before Shelby hit the gas. I texted our numbers to Astrid, who sent back that Nevada's quad was en route and two minutes away. Exact goblin numbers unknown, but they were attacking openly.

This is going to be bad.

Over the years, the Triads had gotten very, very good at hiding the existence of vampires and other species from the general public. Mutilated bodies blamed on animal attacks, unexplained events pushed under the rug by the police officers on our payroll.

The Watchtower didn't have those cops in place, and with goblins attacking more and more openly, it was getting harder to hide them. It would next to impossible this time. Rufus was good, but even he couldn't take down every single photo or YouTube video in time. Not before something went viral.

It's the end of the world as we know it.

And I felt sick to my stomach. So far from fine it wasn't even funny.

Less than three minutes from the mall, another group text chimed over. The hilarity of ten people checking their phones at once was totally lost to the image I brought up on my screen, along with a simple sentence: *These aren't goblins.*

The photo made my insides clench. The same size and general shape as a goblin, with shaggy black hair all over its body. The damned things looked like chimps from Hell, and their eyes burned red.

"What the fuck is that?" someone asked.

"A dwarf," I replied.

"Are you kidding?"

"No. Christ." I tried to call Nevada, but he didn't pick up. I sent over a text in case: *Diamonds distract them. Break into a jewelry store or something.*

He'd probably think I was crazy, but I had to try. I had no idea if Wyatt had shared his information on dwarves and fairies with anyone except me. And the fact that dwarves, and not goblins, were attacking a mall full of humans meant that this was truly a first blood strike by the Fey.

My phone rang. Wyatt.

This won't be fun.

"Hey, handsome."

"Where are you, Evy?"

Not even a hello. He was pissed. "Almost at the epicenter of our latest disaster, why? Where are you?"

"Getting into a car as we speak. You couldn't have waited?"

"Suck it up, buttercup, I was already near a van loaded with weapons. You'll be here in no time."

"Be careful. Those are dwarves."

"Yeah, no shit. Maybe I'll get to wear that tiara after all."

"I'd pay money to see you kicking ass in a tiara."

"I bet you would. See you soon."

"See you."

Evening traffic across the city had Shelby swearing a blue streak that made me a little envious, and it took way longer than we'd hoped to get across the Black River to the uptown mall. The sight of police cars and emergency lights already near the mall entrances dashed all hope of us getting inside with any ease. The mall's basic shape was a square, with each of the four corners anchored by a big department store, and two main entrances opposite each other. Not counting the four department stores.

Six points of entry and exit.

People were racing out of the entrance nearest us, some of them bloody, others assisting their wounded companions. The cops didn't seem to know what was happening. Four rushed inside, leaving one on the sidewalk to the guard the big glass doors.

"How should we play this?" Shelby asked.

Phineas was wedged into the van near the front and he leaned forward. "With as little violence against humans as possible. Pull up closer. I'll use my wings to distract the officer, so the rest of you can rush inside. I'll join you as soon as possible."

"Sounds like a plan," I said.

I texted Nevada and Astrid that we'd arrived and were about to join the fray. We piled out of the van, an odd assortment of shapes and sizes, all armed to the teeth.

The uniformed cop took one look and his eyes went wide. One hand pressed against his service weapon, while he raised his other in a stop gesture. "We have a situation," he said. "No one's allowed inside."

"We aren't just anyone," I said. "We can deal with your problem."

"How?"

Phineas tugged off his t-shirt, and seconds later a beautiful set of mottled brown and tan wings spanned out on either side of his body.

I jacked a thumb. "That's how."

The cop started stuttering, so I took that our cue to head on inside. He didn't try to stop us.

"I'll get a lay of the land," Phineas said, and then on a hard gust of air, he was flying overhead. Straight toward the sounds of screaming and gunfire.

The entrance emptied into a short corridor of store fronts that had already pulled their gates down. Main power was off, and only a few sparsely placed emergency lights gave us a shadowy idea of how to proceed. A few smears of blood led the way toward the main corridor ahead—the source of all the noise.

"What are they?"

"Just shoot the fucking things!"

"Is that a goddamn angel?"

"What's going on?"

The city's finest were freaking the fuck out.

I separated my butterfly swords. We turned the corner and walked into a war zone.

Broken store front windows. Glass all over. Pools of blood. Mangled human bodies next to the occasional dead dwarf. Fake plants knocked over. A blue-tiled fountain held a dead body that was turning the water red. The familiar stench of old seawater that came with goblin blood, which only solidified the fact that the two species were related.

"There's a bunch of people cornered in the food court!" Nevada's voice carried from somewhere ahead.

We were close to the food court, so our group started to run. Someone's flashlights—probably the police—bounced off walls. Boone paused long enough to spear a writhing dwarf in the head with his machete. The sight of fighting ahead urged me faster, and the sudden slam of a body into mine knocked me onto my ass. Everyone started shouting at once as more small, hairy bodies flung themselves out of a candy store and at our group.

A hair-covered face snarled at me, its red eyes burning with hate even in the dim light. I buried a sword into the side of that thing's head to the hilt. Blood spurted on my hand and dribbled out of its mouth. I shoved it aside, a little grossed out that dwarves apparently liked to run around totally naked, and the shaggy hair didn't do a lot to cover the gnarly bits.

I speared one that had Boone on the ground, then helped him up. Blood smeared his shoulder but he wasn't gushing red yet. All around us, the dwarves lay in bits and pieces, easily killed despite the ambush. None of my people were dead, so I called it a win.

"Keep moving," I said.

"Someone help us!" a woman screamed.

I directed two of my people toward the sound, which was coming from a lingerie store, with a terse, "Get them outside."

The rest of us plunged forward, through a dark mall, toward the chaos of the food court, which was at the interior of the mall. It only had one way in from the main corridor, and as we turned, the scene made my gut roll.

At least fifty people were crowded into the back of the food court, huddled together against different counters, many of them wounded. A small army of dwarves stood between the humans and the combined Watchtower/police forces. The cops were holding their batons instead of their guns, probably so they didn't accidentally shoot a bystander, and it was quickly clear that everyone was deferring to Nevada.

One of the original Triad Handlers, he was a solidly-built guy with a background in the Marines, and the man knew how to handle a crowd. My group joined the line, and I sidled up next to Nevada.

"Nice to see some backup," he said.

"What's going on?"

"We're at a standoff here. Every time we move forward, some of them moves toward the hostages. I have two people still clearing the rest of the mall, but there are probably more innocents that need help."

"We were attacked by a pocket of dwarves on the way in." I sent Boone and Nestor off to help clearing the mall. Plus Phineas wasn't here yet so he was probably flying people to safety.

The image almost made me smile.

"We can't stand here all night," Shelby said. "We need to end this before more police show up. Explaining ourselves to a SWAT team isn't high on my to-do list."

"Mine either," I said. "I can teleport to the other side of the dwarf line with up to three people."

"You can?" a nearby cop asked. She was young, her smooth face spackled with red, and she was holding her baton with shaking hands. "That's impossible."

"Sweetie, you're staring at a few dozen dwarves, and not all of my people are human. Trust me, it's not impossible."

She paled.

Was I ever that innocent?

A ruckus and an echoing cat roar told me more backup had arrived. Moments later, Astrid, in full spotted leopard mode, stole into the room. One of the cops screamed and reached for their gun. She disappeared into the shadows of one of the restaurants, followed quickly by the golden lioness that was probably Lynn.

Phineas flew into the room, staying high near the ceiling, his muscled chest splattered fuchsia. Wyatt, Jackson, and five others joined the line. Wyatt was already in half-beast mode, and the female cop near us nearly fell over when she saw him.

His bi-shift wasn't sexy at all, but power thrummed off of him like a live wire.

"Oh good, you can come with me," I told him.

"Where are we going?"

"You, me and two other volunteers are gonna teleport to the space between the dwarves and the very scared people, so that we can finally engage and end this."

Wyatt glanced at Nevada, who nodded his agreement. Kyle and Shelby quickly volunteered. We moved to the back of the crowd, so I could concentrate. Teleporting hurt every time, but at least we weren't teleporting through anything solid. That hurt like a motherfucker. Thirty feet through empty air was a cakewalk next to some of the things I'd teleported through in the past.

I picked my location, sheathed my butterfly swords, and then got everyone to stand in a circle, holding hands. Wyatt was on my right, Kyle on my left. "This is gonna feel weird." I closed my eyes and sought the Break. That magical tether that allowed my unique power to work.

It tried to hide from me, hovering just out of reach. Either a Fey trick or we weren't very close to a Break source, I didn't know or care. I caught a tendril of magic, then reached for my emotional tap. Loneliness was hard to find in such a crowd, so I focused on the idea of Phineas going to his death tomorrow. On Marcus leaving Milo behind, and that was enough. My connection snapped to life, and a hot tingling sensation spread through my body. I imagined our destination in my mind, and then we were moving.

Four people—human and other—were taken apart by magic and put back together again on the other side. I fell to my knees, dizzy and in pain, oblivious to the eruption of movement around me. It took a lot of energy to teleport with that much baggage.

Human hands grabbed me and pulled, and I let them yank me away from the surge of fighting.

"What the fuck? Chalice?"

I blinked a kind-of-familiar face into focus. A young man was staring at me like he'd found his long-lost sister. "Huh?"

"It's me. Shawn? We worked together at Baxter's Coffee Shop up until this past spring when you went AWOL."

"Oh, hi." I remembered him now. A gangly, awkward kid who's recognized Chalice on the street outside the Fourth Street Library. A lifetime ago. I'd told some quick lie to get him away from me, and now the poor guy was a dwarf hostage.

Now that I'd found my center again, I surveyed the battle raging. Astrid and Lynn attacked with vigor, big paws slicing and batting the smaller bodies of the dwarves. Wyatt was doing the same with an almost gleeful snarl on his face. Mostly the police kept to the edges, slipping in to help protect the innocent on my side of the line.

"Are you some kind of ninja?" Shawn asked.

I almost laughed. "Something like that. Keep your head down, okay?"

"Chalice—?"

I pulled my swords, snapped them apart, and plunged into the battle. Blood spurted. Furry bodies piled up around us. They had us outnumbered, but these dwarves weren't trained in battle. All they knew was instinct. Amalie had sent them to die by our hand, and I'm sure she'd done it without remorse.

The death toll didn't matter for her. She'd delivered first blood, and we were openly fighting Dregs in front of the innocent. All of the things we'd tried to hide from the public were being recorded on cell phones by a brave few, and by tomorrow, nothing would be the same.

Phineas swooped overhead, his wing beats gusting the air around me. He dove in to assist where needed, occasionally flinging a dwarf at the ceiling for fun. He moved like the battle-worn warrior he was, uncaring of his audience, knowing that victory was our only option.

I surged onward, delivering death blows as needed, the stink of dead dwarves making my stomach churn. The blood coating my bare skin and clothes felt like the worst kind of slime, and I wanted it off me. Adrenaline kept me moving. Utter exhaustion of killing and fighting put an awful taste in my mouth, and several times I swallowed back the urge to vomit.

Someone screamed nearby. I spun, seeking the source. Two dwarves had the female police officer on the ground. I charged at them. Her vest seemed to be protecting her torso from the worst of their claws, but her neck and face were bleeding. I swung hard with both hands, plunging my swords into the backs of their necks. Simultaneously severing their spines. Both collapsed on top of the cop.

I helped her roll them off, then extended a hand. She took it with a firm grip, breathing hard but somehow not panicking like I expected.

"What are they? Really?" she asked.

"They're the stuff of nightmares," I replied.

"What are you?"

"Same answer." I glanced at her name tag. "Watch your back, Officer Hendrix."

Only a handful of dwarves were still alive, and they'd be dead very soon, judging by the way Astrid and Lynn were sneaking up in their position. My people were joining the cops in a defensive perimeter around the innocents. As I passed Nevada, I shouted out, "Gonna do more recon and make sure the mall is clear."

He saluted his understanding.

Wyatt would snarl about me running off alone, and that was a problem for later. Swords at the ready, I stuck to the center of the corridor and picked my way down the west side of the mall. Many store fronts were closed, gates down. If the workers were still inside, they were doing a fantastic job of hiding.

One length down, and no signs of dwarves or my people—not counting the occasional dead dwarf.

Glad I don't have to clean this mess up.

The mall was going to be closed for a while.

A group text from Rufus came through: *Cops have sealed off the mall, no one going in or out until they can assess what's happening inside.*

Good news for us. Fewer cops inside meant fewer chances of one of us getting accidentally shot.

In the distance someone screamed. I charged forward, taking the next right into a new corridor. At least a dozen dead humans scattered the ground in front of me, their bodies ripped and gaping. The larger concentration of deaths suggested I was close to the start of the slaughter. The heavy odors of blood and death suffocated me.

I picked my way around the dead, avoiding puddles of blood and bits of flung gore. I didn't want to be there anymore but lives depended on quick action. Someone had screamed and they might still be alive.

A shadow moved. I slowed to a crawl until the moving object came into focus. A wounded dwarf was crawling on its belly, useless legs dragging behind it. As much as I wanted to hate the beast, to leave it to suffer a slow death, the dwarf was only a soldier following orders. All of these dwarves were on a suicide mission, whether they wanted to kill or not. The creature on the ground might be my enemy but I didn't have to be cruel.

I pierced its spine, and it went still. A quick death.

As I picked my way forward, I killed three more dying dwarves and stumbled over two more human corpses. The death toll of innocents would make me cry if I thought about it too hard, so I didn't. I kept moving, seeking. Listening for clues.

A low moan came from the interior of a clothing store. The emergency light gave me very little work with as I picked my way around racks of overpriced clothing no one would want to wear in four months anyway. Past two dead dwarves.

"Who's there?"

Boone.

I rushed forward. He was on his back near another dead dwarf, both hands pressing a shirt against his abdomen. Sweaty and pale, he looked at me with pleading eyes. I yanked another shirt off a hanger and dropped to my knees. "How bad?"

"Bad."

I texted an alert of my location and that I needed help ASAP. "We'll get you out of here, okay?"

"Can't host."

"What?" I tried to pay attention to him but I couldn't let my guard down. Couldn't stop scanning the room.

"Demon. I'm jacked up. Can't host like this."

"Fuck the demon, pal. Concentrate on staying alive, okay?"

He wasn't coughing up blood, which gave me a smidge of extra hope. I hadn't known Boone long, but he was a fierce fighter and super-protective of his Clan.

"We took care of the dwarves in the food court," I said. "Saved a bunch of people but the cops are so confused right now I almost feel sorry for them."

Boone shook his head. "Don't. They've seen things. They pretend they don't but they do."

He was probably right about that.

Two sets of footsteps moving fast in our direction put my hackles up, until Jackson and Wyatt appeared in the dim store. Wyatt was back to man-mode, and he did a silent assessment of the damage. Jackson disappeared into the back of the store, using his phone as a flashlight. A minute later, something squealed its way toward us.

Jackson pushed some sort of flat metal cart over to Boone. It was big enough to hold him with his knees bent, so between the three of us we got him arranged on the cart. Wyatt pushed it into the corridor.

"Do we have an exit strategy yet?" I asked.

"North exit has the least amount of cops right now," Wyatt replied. "It's also where all of our vehicles are, so it's our best chance of getting out without too much violence."

"Too much violence?"

"The cops are going to want answers that we can't give them."

"Joy."

By the time we made it to the north entrance, all of our people had reassembled. Some were wounded, and everyone was blood-splattered. Thankfully most of it was fuchsia, not red. Astrid and Lynn had shifted back and were wearing clothes that still had price tags attached. The one face that surprised me was Officer Hendrix. She was talking to Nevada and Astrid, flashing red and blue lights from outside washing over them.

Time to insert myself into the conversation.

"—what happened or who you people are," Hendrix said, "but you saved a lot of lives. Thank you."

"This shouldn't have happened," Astrid said. "I wish I could explain what's going on, but I can't. You'll sleep better at night not knowing."

"I understand."

"I have wounded that I need to take out of here."

Hendrix glanced at the exit. "I'll do what I can to help that happen."

"That's much appreciated. We don't have time to stand around answering questions. All your fellow officers need to know is that lives were saved. You and your companions were very brave in the face of so much confusion."

She smiled. "Thank you, ma'am."

Hendrix led the way toward the entrance and, for a moment, I thought the fading red and blue lights were my imagination. By the time we reached the glass exit doors, we were watching the taillights of three police cars driving away.

"What the hell?" I said.

Wyatt's phone pinged. He laughed as he read the message. "Good old Rufus hacked into the police communications board and had all cars move away from this location to the south side."

"Smart man."

"Glad he's on our side."

"Says the man who once locked the poor guy in a freezer."

Wyatt shrugged. "At the time he deserved it."

Hendrix looked at us both like we were crazy.

Maybe we were, a little bit. After all of the insane shit we'd seen and done in our short lives, we deserved to go a little mad sometimes.

CHAPTER SEVEN

11:15

"We're going to need another volunteer to host," Astrid said.

Her announcement didn't surprise me at all, nor did it seem to surprise any of the other two dozen Watchtower members in the War Room. Astrid stood at the head of the U-shaped table with Marcus and Phineas flanking her, both of their expressions completely neutral.

Okay, so not totally neutral. Marcus looked perkier than he had in weeks, despite having completely missed out on the battle at the mall.

Elder Rojay was the only Clan Elder in the room, and his quiet stoicism probably kept Astrid's words from sending anyone into a panic. "How long do we have to find a replacement?" he asked.

"About eight hours," she replied.

It was almost eight o'clock, and we were doing this around six tomorrow morning. This was totally cutting it close.

"However," Astrid continued, "if we don't get a third volunteer, then the elves will only summon two Tainted."

"Won't our odds be better with all three?" Wyatt asked, his voice still unnaturally growly and deep.

"Of course they will, but we can't force anyone into making this choice."

Boone was alive but he wasn't going to be part of the demon army tomorrow, which meant someone else had to make the agonizing decision to take his place.

I squeezed Wyatt's wrist, mostly to keep him grounded. He was still wound up from the fight. His Lupa side reveled in the bloodshed and destruction, and he had a harder time coming down from that after each new battle.

"As for what happened at the mall," Astrid continued, "we can't save it. Too many people, too many smartphones. One video of Phineas tossing dwarves around like popcorn has already been shared ten-thousand times. In less than three hours. Rufus tried but it's out there. Along with a lot of your faces."

Oh great.

"So for right now, anyone who was at the mall tonight is forbidden from leaving the Watchtower until it's necessary for us to engage the Fey. Is that understood?"

House arrest. Lovely. I nodded along with everyone else. It's not as if I had anyplace to be before Armageddon.

Astrid surveyed the room full of nodding heads before saying, "Dismissed." And then adding, "Truman? A word in private?"

With Wyatt still high from battle lust, no way was I doing anything except sticking close as the rest of the War Room emptied out. Astrid barely glanced at me as she put herself in front of Wyatt, shoulders back, a stance that suggested she was about to say something he wouldn't like.

"Bi-shifters are the strongest candidates for hosting a Tainted," she said. "It's why Boone volunteered, and why Phineas is one of our best choices. After speaking with Brevin, he agrees with me that Lupa boys are our next strongest options."

"No," Wyatt snapped with no hesitation, on the same breath that I said, "Fuck that."

Anger rolled off of Wyatt like a physical force, and in his completely silver eyes I saw impending violence. I grabbed his bicep and held tight.

"They're teenagers," I said, trying my hand at being Wyatt's voice of reason for once. "Even if they're physically strong enough to endure a demon, they don't know how to fight. They're terrified of almost everyone in his place. How the hell do you expect them to engage in an actual battle?"

"I'm broaching a discussion," Astrid said. "Brevin handed me a fact, and I'm acting on it."

"There is no discussion." Wyatt yanked out of my grip and crossed his arms. His steely determination made my insides watery. "None of the boys will be housing a Tainted. I volunteer."

"What?" I squawked. "You are not."

He wouldn't look at me, the bastard. "I have to."

"No you don't." I grabbed his cheeks with both hands and forced him to look at me. With silver hiding his eyes, his emotions were harder to see, and I kind of hated him for that. I hated him for making this split-second decision without discussing it me first. He hadn't given me a chance to talk him out of it, and even as I stared at the face of a man I loved with my whole heart, I knew he was right.

Something deep inside me churned, burning hot and freezing cold all at once. Understanding that, in some ways, everything had led us to this moment in time. Every choice we made, every decision that had influenced us over the last six months. From the murders of Jesse and Ash to Wyatt's infection, to tonight's battle at the mall. Every drop of blood we shed, every tear we wiped away, was for this.

Preparation for the final battle that would decide our fates, not only as a couple, but as a species.

"I hate you for this," I said, my voice as hollow as my heart.

"I know you do." Wyatt blinked hard and some of his black iris returned, ringed in silver. "I hate myself for doing it."

"You're half-human," Astrid said.

"I'm also half-Lupa and losing more of myself to that part every time I bi-shift. Every time I kill for the wolf inside of me."

She studied him with a bizarre mix of fear and respect. "Brevin will have to agree."

"Then ask him." Those words came out on a terrifying growl. "But it won't be the boys."

"Okay. I'll ask."

Astrid left the room to do just that, leaving me alone with Wyatt. As alone as we could be with Ops going full-steam on the other side of the wall. I couldn't seem to let go of Wyatt's face. Couldn't move at all, except for the faint trembling in my fingers.

Trembling he recognized, and his entire face softened. "I'm sorry."

"Don't apologize." I let him wrap me tight against his chest, my own palms flat to his shoulders. Unable to hold him back. "I actually do understand why you have to do this."

"You do?"

"A few months ago, I wouldn't have. I never used to believe in fate, or that things worked out a certain way for a reason, but you changed that in me. Your constant support and love changed that." I raised my head to hold eye contact, because this was important. "I believe that Phin came crashing down on that car and scared us to death for a reason. I believe that Marcus chose to defend his people as a warrior rather than as a father for a reason. I believe that you died and rose again and were bitten by the Lupa for a fucking reason. And I believe the three of you will lead us to victory tomorrow."

Gentle adoration shone in Wyatt's eyes, and his mouth quirked into a smile. "Knowing you believe it makes me believe it, too."

"Good. Now we just need to make sure both Milo and Phineas's mystery lover believe it with their whole hearts."

"Make sure who believes what?" Phineas strode over from the entrance to Ops. Blood-free and in clean clothes, he watched us both with his head slightly cocked. "What going on?"

I couldn't make myself say it. The words got stuck in my throat.

"Astrid said that after your kind, the Lupa were the next strongest choice as a Tainted host," Wyatt said. "So I volunteered."

Phineas blinked hard several times, his shock almost comical because I'd never seen Phineas at a loss for words. He stared, lips pressed together, until I shifted my weight and his gaze dropped to me. His surprise turned to confusion. "And you haven't talked him out of it?"

Part of me wanted to. I wanted to take Wyatt and the boys and get the hell out of dodge before tomorrow morning, final battle be damned. But I knew neither of us could have lived with ourselves if we did that. Wyatt had been there at the start of Amalie's deceptions, which led all the way back to the formation of the Triads. He wouldn't leave, and I would never ask him to.

Not after everything we'd been through.

"Don't faint," I said, "but I agree with him."

"You do."

"Yes. He's half-Lupa. He can bi-shift. He carries the blood line of a very strong, ancient race. He's also Gifted, so he's connected to the Break. He can do this." I reached out and brushed my fingers lightly across Phin's cheek. "All three of you can."

His fierce expression softened a fraction. "You are so unlike the woman I first met many months ago, Evangeline. Your spirit is stronger, your resolve more intact. You think with your heart *and* your head. I am honored to be your friend." He looked past me to Wyatt. "And yours."

I half-expected Wyatt to growl. Instead, he extended his right hand. Phineas shook it in a sure grip, and my love for both of those men compounded.

"Brevin has to agree," Wyatt said.

Phineas nodded. "He will. You are the logical choice."

A wash of pride flooded me. "And all three of you will have an army at your backs," I said. "Shifters and humans, and if we're lucky, the vampires will be able to assist us."

"Has anyone spoken to Eulan recently? Or Omal? Will the vampires join us?"

Someone behind us cleared their throat. "We will," said a familiar female voice.

I spun out of Wyatt's arms, a shot of joy carrying me the six long strides to where Isleen stood in the War Room doorway. She held tightly to Quince's arm, another face was I crazy happy to see back at the Watchtower, and I froze before I actually did something ridiculous like try to hug her. Her complexion was nearly snow white, paler than any normal vampire, and she listed slightly, as though unsteady on her feet.

She probably was, and doing her damnedest not to show weakness. Thackery's virus had changed the infected vampires irrevocably. Isleen and the others were alive, but they were forever weakened.

"I am so fucking happy to see you," I said, my words for both of them.

"Likewise, Evangeline," Isleen said with a ghost of a smile on her lips. "When I went to sleep for the last time, I did not honestly expect to awaken in this world. I hear our survival is by your hand."

"No, it wasn't me. An Apothi I know gave me the potion that saved your lives. All I did was deliver it."

"After a lengthy battle and at great cost." Her smile dimmed. "I am so sorry for the loss of your friend."

My heart ached but I pushed it away. "Thank you. So your Families have agreed to help?"

"They have," Quince said. "It didn't take as much convincing from Eulan as you'd expect. Our Fathers know what is at stake should the Fey succeed in wiping out mankind. We would very likely be next. This war will only be won if we band together. Vampire, Therian, human."

"Glad they figured that one out before the ball dropped."

He blinked. "What ball?"

"Never mind."

"To bring a Tainted across the Break is an enormous risk," Isleen said. "Your folklore calls my people monsters, but the Tainted are far worse. They are emotion and power and the thing of nightmares. If they are not contained properly, then we'll have done the Fey's work for them."

"We are well aware," Phineas said.

Isleen held his gaze a beat, then those lavender eyes met mine. "Do you trust the word of this elf Brevin, despite what his kin attempted?"

"I do." My lack of hesitation in answering must have helped her believe me, because she nodded again. "In a way, Tovin had the right idea but he went about it all wrong."

"And where is the Tainted that Tovin summoned?"

I stared at Isleen, not understanding. Not until Wyatt went tense beside me and said, "Oh shit."

Months ago, Tovin had successfully summoned a Tainted across the Break—but instead of going into me, I dodged that bullet and the Tainted infected Tovin. Between me and Wyatt, we killed Tovin and trapped the Tainted inside of a black crystal prison. Amalie hid it with her kin, only to have it stolen by Walter Thackery. Thackery then ransomed it back to us, and we'd housed it in a lead-lined box at Boot Camp. But Boot Camp didn't exist anymore, and it hadn't for months.

"What happened to everything from Boot Camp?" I asked. With the building of the Watchtower, our pursuit of Thackery, and the looming war with the Fey, I hadn't given much thought to the research and modified weapons that had been taken out of the Research and Development building. "We took the box with us. Did it end up here?"

Wyatt looked at Phineas, who only shrugged.

"Where's Gina?" I asked. "She might know."

"In her room," Phineas replied.

The fact that he knew that made me give him a hard stare. He returned it with is trademark poker face.

Phin and Kismet? Now that's an odd pairing....

Instead of racing all over the universe to find her, I did the logical thing and used my phone. She picked up in the third ring. "Kismet."

"It's Stone. When we were packing up Boot Camp back in July, we got the box that held the Tainted crystal, right?"

"The Tainted crystal? Yes. Adrian had an inventory list of everything we put into storage. What do you need it for?"

"A paperweight." I rolled my eyes, even though she couldn't see it. "I don't need it, but it just occurred to me that we had it."

"Do you think Brevin might find it useful?" Phineas asked.

"I don't know, but let's ask him."

"Ask who what?" Kismet said.

"Never mind," I said to her. "We're in Ops if you want to join the party. Your boyfriend's here, too."

She made a squawking sound that I hung up on. Phineas's poker face stayed on point.

"Brevin has been here for days," Isleen said. "Do you truly believe that no one thought to mention you have a Tainted in containment?"

Only Isleen could make a simple question into a personal barb about my being slower than everyone else to grasp the obvious. So I did a nonchalant shrug. "I don't know. And it's not like I've ever had a sit-down with

Brevin to discuss the particulars of tomorrow morning. I'd forgotten about our crystal-shaped Tainted hostage, that's all."

"You want to help, Evy," Wyatt said. "There's nothing wrong with that."

I grunted. "Isleen's right, though. I'm sure Brevin knows about it. Maybe he can't break the magic around it, or maybe he can't use an already trapped demon. Who knows?"

"You would be correct in that assumption." Brevin's voice made me jump. "While the Tainted's continued entrapment is quite an impressive feat of both magic and human engineering, it has been removed from its power source for too long to be of any real use. The joining to the host would simply not take."

At least that answered that question.

Brevin shuffled toward us, coming to a stop in front of Wyatt. He peered up, his long, narrow face more exaggerated from such an angle, but he studied Wyatt with a sharp gaze. "You are not fully Therian, and yet you wish to take this risk."

"Yes, I do," Wyatt said. "I've overcome great odds, and I've cheated death dozens of times, and I believe in my heart that it was all to bring me to this point in time. This action."

"Good. That belief is what will help you control the being that will become a part of you. Any doubt or fear on your part will allow the Tainted to take control."

"I understand."

I squeezed Wyatt's wrist, mostly to keep myself grounded. So much pride and love filled my heart, and I didn't know what else to do with it. Despite spending the bulk of the past ten years out of the field, directing Hunters, he was as fierce a warrior as anyone else in the Watchtower.

The sudden blaring of the perimeter alarms shattered the meaningful moment.

Now what?

Our entire group, sans Brevin, barreled into Ops. Rufus had an aerial map of the Watchtower grounds up on one of the big monitors, with dozens of tiny blue and red dots all over the building. Humans, Therians and vampires. In the lower left side of the screen, a large cluster of red was moving toward us.

"What is that?" Wyatt asked.

"I'm not sure yet," Rufus replied.

Astrid stormed the room with Marcus and Kyle hot on her heels. "Is it an attack?"

"Unknown." Rufus hit something on the console in front of him, and a second bank of monitors woke up. The six smaller screens flashed various views from exterior security cameras. The mall, the parking lot, even several of the nearby side streets. Other than a stray cat and one passing car, there was nothing.

"There are at least three dozen warm-blooded creatures heading toward us in a group," Astrid said, pointing a finger at the sensor map. "Where the hell are they?"

"The sky," Phineas said. Something in his voice made me look at him. He wasn't worried or angry. Instead, his narrow face held a bizarre kind of relief.

Without a word, he turned and ran. I followed without any real thought, vaguely aware of other footsteps behind me. He headed down the western corridor toward the gym area, then banked a sharp left to the old maintenance rooms and roof access. I half-expected him to rip off his shirt and fly to the top of the ladder, but something had him too excited (or freaked) to bother.

I stayed right on his tail, up the metal ladder that kind of made me dizzy for its straight-up wrungs. He shoved the hatch open and disappeared through it.

"Evy, be careful." Wyatt, below me.

I didn't have any weapons on me, but something deep down told me I wouldn't need any. I climbed through the hatch and swung out onto the gravel-covered roof. Phineas stood near the edge, his wings spread wide, staring south.

And in the light of a nearly full moon, I saw them. Like a heavenly host of angels from on high, dozens of winged men and women were flying toward us, high in the sky and gradually dipping lower. The beauty of their wings stirred the air around us, and all I could do was stand next to Phineas and stare.

"Coni?" Wyatt asked.

Phineas nodded, his bright blue eyes shimmering with emotion.

"I thought you said you didn't find any," I said.

"I didn't." Phineas made a sound that was half-laugh, half-sob. "Someone else did."

He pointed. I followed the trajectory of his finger to a woman flying at the very front of the flock. Long, brown spirals of hair, gorgeous white and gray wings. As she drew closer, I started to laugh, too. And maybe shed a tear or three.

Aurora was home, and she'd brought backup.

CHAPTER EIGHT

10:40

I lost count of the number of Coni who landed on the roof, all in bi-shift, and all wearing very similar outfits. The men were bare-chested, while the women wore what looked like leather bikini tops. All wore knee-length leather pants that disappeared into rustic boots, and I'd have laid money on those clothes behind hand-made. Deadly-looking forged blades hung from their hips by leather straps. They had the same familiar features as Phineas and Aurora—the narrow faces, sharp cheekbones, and piercing blue eyes. Long, wild hair on the women and many of the men.

They were beautiful.

Aurora stepped forward from the flock, her cheeks blazing and panting slightly. I'd seen her in bi-shift only once before, and she looked even more the fierce warrior she'd been that night. She stood with a confidence I didn't remember, power rippling beneath her skin.

She stared at me with open shock. "Evangeline?"

"Surprise," I said.

"You're not dead."

"No, and neither is Marcellus Dane. I'm so sorry you had to see that deception."

She shook her head, blinking hard. Her questions stayed silent, though, because she turned her attention to Phineas. He went to her and swept her smaller body into his arms. Their wings closed around them, as if joining the embrace. Keeping their reunion private for a moment.

Behind them, the other Coni stood silent, staring. They were starting to give me the creeps, so I glanced behind me to see who'd come up. Wyatt, Astrid, Marcus, Quince, and Kismet stood in a wide circle near the roof access.

One of the Coni hissed, and the sound broke up Aurora and Phineas's hug. A tall, black-winged man with inky hair had gone rigid, his attention fixed over my left shoulder.

Wyatt. Coni and Lupa were not a good mix.

I shifted sideways to stand directly in front of Wyatt and bared my own teeth.

Aurora held up a silencing hand, and the man went silent.

Damn, girl.

She approached us with open concern. "I've explained Wyatt's condition to them, but the reaction is very instinctual. They've lived away from mankind for many generations."

"Where did you find them?" Phineas asked. He looked like he was trying very hard not to cry, and I didn't blame him. For a long while, Phineas believed that Aurora's daughter Ava would be the last of the Coni, and now at least three dozen had flown in from gods knew where.

"Greece," Aurora replied. "On a small island in the Sea of Crete."

"You've been gone such a short time. How did you find them?"

"I'll tell you everything, I promise." She looked past us both. "Astrid, may we come inside?"

"Only you for now," Astrid replied. "Everyone else can remain up here with Marcus and Quince."

Aurora nodded. "I appreciate your caution."

By the time we all reconvened in the War Room—plus the addition of Rufus, Kyle, and Paul—my questions were bouncing around in my head like pinballs. No one sat, but Aurora stood at the head of the table like she'd been holding meetings like this her entire life. The shy, terrified were-kestrel I knew from before was gone, replaced by a warrior.

"Where are Ava and Joseph?" I asked.

"I left Ava with trusted friends on the island," Aurora replied, her song-bird voice clear and strong. "She'll be well looked after."

"And Joseph?"

Grief bracketed her eyes. "Joseph lived to the end of his life. He passed three days ago."

Wyatt's arm slid around my waist, and I leaned into him. The news didn't surprise me, but it still hurt.

"How did you find the Coni?" Astrid asked. Business as usual.

"They found us," Aurora said. "When we fled the Dane house, we were uncertain where to go. No place seemed safe, so Joseph and I decided to leave the country entirely. We flew to Europe, occasionally stowing away on freight vessels to rest. Joseph was the one who wanted to see Greece. He said he wanted to live his final days near clear water, eating good food."

The affection in her voice made my throat tighten with unshed tears.

"We spent much of our time in our true forms, flying and fishing and being happy. And then one day we met an eagle that had no business living in Greece. His name was Pike. He's the man with the black wings who hissed at Wyatt."

Wyatt grunted.

"I never expected to meet more Coni, so I was shocked to be brought to their island. Hundreds of our people are there. Many have spent their lives in their true forms, but they remember how to bi-shift. When I explained who we were and what was happening here, a clutch of warriors volunteered to help. After Joseph passed, we began the journey back to this city."

"You did what I could not," Phineas said. "You showed that we are not alone in this world."

Aurora grasped his hand. "Ava has more family than she knows what to do with now. She has a future, Phineas. As does our people."

"I am so proud of you, Aurora. You honor the lives who were lost by your return tonight."

"We're a part of this world. And I will fight to give my daughter the future she deserves." She looked out at the faces watching her and met my gaze. "As I fight for all of us."

"You trust this clutch of warriors?" Astrid asked.

"I do. And you can trust them, too."

"We have three young Lupa who reside here, under the protection of Truman and Stone. Will your warriors respect their lives?"

Aurora's eyes narrowed briefly. "I will take responsibility for my warriors. The Lupa will not be harmed by any of my people."

Behind me, Wyatt relaxed and let out a breath. The boys were having a rough enough time around the young Felia in the Watch. They didn't need the added stress of a bunch of Coni warriors targeting them.

Maybe they need to stay in the apartment for the rest of the night.

Not that they'd stepped foot out since the cafeteria incident, which reminded me that I needed to check in with John. He wasn't handling his captivity memories well, and I knew a little something about post-torture PTSD.

"The warriors may come inside," Astrid said. "The empty room to the left of the gym is large enough to house them, if they wish to rest. I imagine you've had a long journey."

"We have," Aurora replied. "Thank you."

"I'll make sure cots and blankets are delivered there, as well as food."

"Their diets have consisted mostly of raw fish for hundreds of years."

Astrid glanced at Rufus, then said, "We'll see what we can do."

Like what, call for sushi delivery?

Aurora and Phineas hustled out to collect the other Coni.

"I can't believe she's back," I said.

Wyatt turned me to face him. "Neither can I. But it's another check mark in our favor. We've both seen Phineas in action. Him times thirty?"

"That's a fight I can't wait to see." Preferably from the sidelines, but that wasn't happening. Even though I was tired of fighting, tired of the constant battle for our lives, I wasn't sitting this one out. Not when all of my friends—and two of the men I loved most on earth—were going to be out there waging war against the Fey and their allies.

Kismet stalked over and poked Wyatt hard in the chest. "You did not."

Wyatt blinked. "I didn't what?"

"Volunteer, you idiot." She looked equal parts angry and sad. "For the Tainted. Are you suicidal?"

"Not at all. Quite the opposite in fact."

I leaned over to kiss Wyatt's cheek. "You have fun with this. I'll see you in a bit."

"Where are you going?"

"To check on the boys."

Marcus intercepted me just outside of Ops, and I let him lead me to the opposite wall, away from several clusters of people. "Thank you," he said quietly.

I had a good idea what he meant, but I still played dumb. "For what?"

"I may have missed the battle at Briar's Ridge, but staying behind gave me a gift I will never forget. A gift I will fight even harder for in the morning."

So much love and affection burned in his copper eyes that I did something I'd never done before. I flung my arms around his broad shoulders and hugged him. He slipped muscled arms around my waist.

"Thank you for caring for him," I whispered. "He needs it more than he even realizes."

"It's something I've needed as well. I've lived a very lonely life."

I pulled away, then wiped at my own damp eyes. "So have most of us. Funny how we don't find love until the end of the world."

Marcus laughed. "Indeed."

"How's he doing?"

"He's being brave for me, as much as for himself. It wounds him to have to stay behind, instead of being there with us. For all that he's been through, Milo deserves to face this enemy with us."

"Yes, he does. But I bet a part of you is glad he'll be safe and sound and far away from the fighting."

He smiled. "A part, yes. Another part wishes him by my side."

"I can understand that." I had the honor of standing by my lover on the field of battle. "Are you going back to him?"

"Soon. Once the Coni are settled. Brevin has said we'll begin preparations by one o'clock, so I don't have much time."

And he wanted every moment he had. I understood that need far too well. We went our separate ways. Word of Wyatt volunteering must have started making the gossip circuit, because I ignored several sympathetic looks as I made my way back to the apartment.

Mark and Peter were in the living room playing a video game.

"There's a new smell in the air," Peter said over the sound of digital car engines.

"A bunch of Coni warriors flew in from Greece to help us fight tomorrow," I said.

Both of them stared at me a beat, then went back to the game.

Teenagers.

Their bedroom door was shut, so I knocked once before entering. John sat on the floor in one corner of the messy room, knees drawn up to his chest. He wasn't rocking or shaking or doing anything much, besides staring at the far wall. I shut the door, then knelt in front of him.

"John?"

His gaze slowly rose to meet mine. He was too fucking young for all of the fear and anxiety in his eyes. "Does it ever stop?"

My heart flipped. "Does what ever stop?"

"The bad dreams? The memories? The pain?"

"In time it becomes less." I shifted to sit next to him. He leaned against me, and I wrapped a comforting arm around his slim shoulders. "I wish I could say it will go away like it never happened, but that's a lie. All you can do is work through it."

"How?"

"Have you talked to anyone about your time with Vale?"

He shook his head.

That surprised me a bit. "Not Wyatt? Or Dr. Vansis?"

"No."

I angled my left hand so he could see it. "A few months ago I was tortured by a man in the name of science. He did awful things, including cutting off my pinkie to see if it would grow back."

John's eyes went wide. "Oh wow. Oh God. You don't act like you were tortured."

"That's because there's no one way to act after suffering through acts of violence. I had people around me who loved me, and who helped me overcome all of the bad things I was feeling. Do you trust me and Wyatt to help you?"

He held my gaze for a long moment before nodding. "Vale told me my brothers were dead. That he killed them and left them for you to find."

My heart ached for the pain in his words.

"I didn't want to believe him. I still felt them, but I was so scared. I was so sure I was going to die, too."

I didn't know what to say to that, so I held him close and listened while this teenage boy—someone I'd come to care for despite myself—opened up and told me about his worst nightmare.

Wyatt found us an hour later. John had fallen asleep with his head on my shoulder after exhausting himself talking. It was probably his first real rest in over a week, so I didn't move. Even after my ass went numb from sitting on the concrete floor. Wyatt carefully picked him up and tucked him into bed. John mumbled once, then passed back out.

In the privacy of our room, Wyatt asked, "What was that?"

I told him. Some of the details enraged Wyatt, as I knew they would, but the anger left quickly. It had no direction, no enemy left to fight. Vale died in many pieces, and his accomplices had been executed by the Assembly for treason. All we could do was support John, until the nightmares dimmed and the world seemed a little less terrifying.

No small feat when every other race on the planet had reason to fear you.

"Thank you," he said. "For reaching out to him."

"I have more experience with kidnapping and torture than most."

He pulled me into his arms, and I went willingly. I rested my cheek on his shoulder and inhaled his scent. Masculine, a hint of cinnamon, and the deeper, muskier smell of his wolf. His heart beat steadily against my chest.

"Promise me something," I said.

"Anything within my power."

"When this is over, when the Fey are done attacking us, and the Tainted are back across the Break? You and me. A tropical beach. Fruity drinks with umbrellas in them."

"Vacation?"

I lifted my head to hold his gaze. "I'm thinking more like a permanent retirement."

His lips twitched. "If we want to stay there forever, we need to find a beach near a Break source."

"Sounds good to me."

"You do realize that if we're near a Break, we won't be the only supernatural beings around."

"Don't care. As long as we're far away from this fucking city."

Wyatt tilted his head. "What about our friends?"

"They can visit whenever they want. I'm tired of fighting, Wyatt. I feel like I've been fighting for my entire life, and I'm exhausted. I want to go someplace with you and not think for a while. To sit in the sun, drink fruity cocktails, and make love to you."

"I like this future of ours." He nuzzled my cheek with his nose. "Especially the last part."

"Sitting in the sun."

He kissed my cheek. "Nope."

"Fruity cocktails?"

"Try again."

I licked my lips, anticipation tightening my belly. "Making love?"

"Yes, please."

We did, with a tender slowness that drew me to the brink of tears over and over. I savored every touch, every kiss, every taste, every orgasm. Every moment we shared together, moving together. No matter how much we believed in a positive outcome, the future wasn't a promise. We couldn't predict what dawn would bring.

All we had was now.

As the time drew closer to midnight, we reluctantly left our bed for the shower. We were both dressed in black cargo pants and shirts, debating a quick trip to the cafeteria, when Wyatt's phone rang.

"Truman." His expression remained neutral. "On our way."

I didn't wait for him to hang up before asking, "Is it time?"

He nodded. "Soon. We've reached the room below Olsmill." The room where Tovin had successfully brought a Tainted into the world via a pool of black water somehow directly linked to First Break. A doorway to another world entirely.

A doorway we were deliberately opening for a second time.

The corridor outside of Ops was jammed with just about every warm body in the building—human, vampire and Therian. We still had squads in the city patrolling, but the bulk of our forces were here. The masses parted for me and Wyatt, which was a little disconcerting. We got a lot of looks, too. Everything from sympathetic to respectful.

Milo was at one of the Ops terminals with headphones on. He met my gaze and winked, an unexpected lightness in his expression. Getting lucky definitely changed a person's perspective on the end of the world.

We made it into the War Room without incident, which held fewer folks than I expected. Astrid and Marcus, Rufus and Kismet, Isleen and Eulan (the first time I'd ever seen them together), plus Phineas, Brevin and a second elf. Identical to Brevin except for his thicker ear hair, the newcomer leaned on a cane of gnarled wood.

Once we were inside, Marcus pulled closed the rarely-used set of doors for the War Room, giving us complete privacy.

Brevin stood on one of the chairs. "It is time to begin preparations for the summoning of three Tainted. My brother, Sorvin, has joined us, and by the time we reach the pool, our other brother will be with us."

"Who three are to be the hosts?" Sorvin asked.

Wyatt squeezed my hand before releasing it. He moved to stand with Phineas and Marcus, the three of them set away from the rest of us. Presenting themselves like pageant finalists waiting for their placements to be called.

Sorvin studied them. "Coni. Felia." He tilted his head at Wyatt. "You are unique."

"I am," Wyatt replied, his voice strong and sure. "I am a Gifted human, as well as of Lupa blood. I embrace both sides of myself, and I'm willing to fight for control of this world."

"Acceptable." To all three of them, Sorvin said, "We cannot promise anything to you. You may all die for your trouble. Do you accept that outcome?"

All three men spoke in unison: "I do."

Sounded like one of the most fucked up wedding vows ever.

Brevin addressed the entire group. "We six will descent into the Break point alone. There can be no distractions while we prepare. The vessels must be focused, ready and willing to accept their burdens. Anything less may prove disastrous."

I bit back a protest. Watching Wyatt leave, knowing what he was about to do and not being able to be by his side hurt. A lot. A physical ache in my gut that knew this might be the last time I saw my Wyatt Truman alive and well. But we had, in many ways, said goodbye earlier.

Someone's fingers curled around mine. I hadn't seen Kismet move, and I squeezed her hand. She'd known Wyatt for nine years. They'd been good friends long before I landed in his lap. We both had our own pain, and for the first time in my adult life, I felt no shame in sharing my pain with another person. No embarrassment in knowing my emotions were plainly written on my face.

I'd never been the heart-on-my-sleeve type.

I'd also never been in love before.

And for some reason, Brevin was looking right at me.

"I understand," I said. "I know my reputation precedes me, but I'll do whatever it takes for this to go in our favor."

Brevin tilted his head in some kind of nod. "We will begin in the darkest moments before dawn. Many will feel the shift in the Break's power the moment the first Tainted crosses, including the Fey. In that moment, we will have declared war upon Amalie and her followers."

Bring it on.

CHAPTER NINE

06:45

We didn't say good-bye. For all we didn't know about the future, neither one of us wanted to jinx it.

I walked with Wyatt to the parking area, hand in hand, saying nothing. There wasn't anything to say. We loved each other. We were both prepared to fight tooth and claw to come back to each other. That was everything.

A lot of people were in the corridor to watch. I didn't care why, be it for the spectacle of two elves, two Therians and a half-breed about to take on the Fey, or for moral support. It didn't matter. The only thing that mattered to me was that three people I loved were heading into uncertainty, and I didn't know if they'd come home whole.

It had already been decided that Aurora and her clutch of Coni warriors would go ahead to keep an eye on the above-ground area, along with Leigh, Jackson and Nevada. The rest of us would wait until dawn to mobilize.

Phineas, the secretive jerk, walked alone. Head held high, shoulders straight. Whoever this mysterious lady love was, she kept herself hidden. Maybe they'd already said what needed to be said. I hugged him hard, memorizing his lean, muscled frame. The odd way his body was both strong and somehow light.

"How far we've come, Evangeline," he said quietly. "From me tricking you into a devil's bargain, to you wishing me well into war."

"It's a war we'll win," I replied. "We have to. I have plans for afterward."

He smiled. "Oh?"

"Yes. A beach. Fruity drinks. No more fighting. God knows I'm owed that much."

"You are owed that much and more. You do your species proud."

"So do you." I kissed his cheek. "Go get a demon and kick some Fey ass."

"Until we meet again."

I turned away, eyes stinging a little, in time to catch a very hot kiss between Marcus and Milo, and in front of everyone. I gave a few people the stink eye, daring them to comment, and they got over it. Kismet came up to hug Milo when the pair had to part ways. I wanted to hug them both—not my default mode, either—but I had one more person to see off first.

Wyatt cupped my cheeks in his palms, skin so warm and familiar. I gazed into his simmering black eyes, with their silver flecks. Eyes that had looked at me as something more than just a Hunter, more than just another sarcastic problem to solve, long before I ever had a clue. This man loved me more than I deserved, and that was what would see us both through this.

We'd been at war since my resurrection. So far we had only been surviving it.

Today we were finally, truly fighting back.

"I'll see you out there," I said.

He seemed to fight against so many things, warring with the part of himself that wanted to say "fuck it" and run as far away as possible. And as lovely as that fantasy was, it would never happen. Neither one of us had ever backed down from a fight. We would both see this through to the end.

"Be careful," Wyatt said.

I laughed. "Always am."

"Be careful anyway."

"You, too, jackass."

His lips twitched. "I thought I was a dumbass."

"You're my ass." I pressed one hand over his heart. "And my heart. Come back to me."

"I will. I love you, Evy Stone."

"I love you too. Always."

I stood alone, arms rigid by my sides, as the van drove off, carrying a large piece of me with it. I stood there long after the crowd broke up and drifted away, many with nothing to do but wait for dawn. I stared at the empty parking lot beyond the magic barrier that pretended to be an intact wall, unable to make my feet move.

My skin prickled with the proximity of another person. "We'll get them back," Milo said.

I turned my head and blinked hard. Sheer determination sparked in his eyes. Not even the walker he gripped made him look less than positive of his desired outcome. I had no idea what my face displayed, but I fed from his confidence. "Yes, we will." I poked him in the shoulder. "Come on, Gimpy. I'm hungry and I want company."

He chuckled. "Wyatt wear you out?"

"Yes, and something tells me I'm not the only one worn out from sex."

Milo blushed.

I planted a kiss on his cheek. "Congrats, by the way."

"Shut up."

"No, I mean it." I grabbed the side of his walker so he couldn't hobble away. "Having something to fight for besides duty and honor? It's that final burst that gets you through, even when you're positive you don't have anything left to give."

He held my gaze for a long moment before nodding. "Thanks for giving us both that extra push."

"Thank me by giving details."

"No, and hell no."

I stuck my tongue out at him. "Spoil sport."

"Brat."

I goaded him the entire way to the cafeteria, because for a little while, it felt really nice to be normal twenty-somethings again.

Even if it wouldn't last.

A little after two in the morning, Astrid called me down to Ops. Her tone of voice told me before I even walked into the command center that I wasn't going to like the news. She and Rufus were bent over a computer terminal, and I got a small twinge of satisfaction at sneaking up on them both.

"Whatever it is, I didn't do it," I said.

"I know you didn't." Astrid's weary tone warned me to back off the sarcasm. "One of our city patrols found a body. They think it's a gnome."

My stomach flipped. "Do they know who it is?"

"No, but I was wondering if you do." She moved to the side so I could see the computer screen.

The pear-shaped body and bald head were familiar, crumpled on what looked like black tar. His throat was slashed, green blood long since dried. My heart ached for the violent death of a creature who'd only ever tried to help me and had now paid the price. "Fuck," I said. "It's Horzt. The gnome who gave me the vampire cure and the elf scroll."

"Carly said the word 'traitor' was written nearby in his blood."

"I thought the gnomes left the city. Horzt said they were leaving."

"Perhaps he stayed behind so his people wouldn't be targeted for his actions," Rufus said.

"Maybe. Where was he found?"

"Under the Lincoln Street Bridge."

The last place I spoke with Horzt. "Then it's definitely a message for us." Another innocent life taken because of contact with me. "Did they find anything else at the scene? Any indication of who killed him?"

Rufus shook his head. "All we know is he was killed elsewhere. There isn't enough blood at the scene for him to have died there."

"So he was put there as another 'fuck you' to me? Nice."

"This isn't your fault, Stone," Astrid said.

I snorted hard. "Yes, it is. Horzt only ever helped us, and now he's dead."

"He made the choice to help you. You didn't ask him to cure the vampires' illness. He offered it of his own free will. He had to have known the risks in going against the other Fey, so you don't get to keep all the guilt on this one."

"And to be honest," Rufus added, "the fact that this is the only major incident since the mall attack is very suspicious."

"What do you mean?" I asked.

"Usually we're monitoring dozens of police calls about strange attacks or incidents that could be Dreg related, especially Halfies or goblins. But tonight's been very…quiet. Considering what happened this morning at the salvage yard, it's not like the goblins to go quiet. Not after they've been so active lately."

"You think the queens are planning something?"

"It's likely." He pinched the bridge of his nose. "The problem is we have no way of knowing until they strike."

I groaned. "Hey, I was all for napalming the sewers weeks ago, but you guys said it wasn't practical."

Rufus's lips twitched. "It's too bad Thackery couldn't have put his genius to better use and developed something to kill goblins, instead of vampires."

"Co-sign, my friend."

Brilliant scientist that he was, Thackery let his blind hatred of the vampires color his vision against useful applications of his research. He'd tried to eradicate the wrong damned species. We'd recovered a bunch of his research materials months ago, but as far as I knew, our own brain trust hadn't been able to piece together anything useful. Apparently he wrote a lot it down in code that no one had cracked yet.

"Do you think they'll hit a major target like the dwarves did?" I asked.

"It's likely," Astrid said. "This Nessa seems quite adamant about justice for the queen you killed."

"Yeah, well, Kelsa kidnapped and tortured me first. Killing her was the least I could do."

"No one's faulting you for that, Stone. We're just being vigilant about—"

Perimeter alarms blared to life for the second time tonight.

"Now what?" I asked.

Rufus switched his monitor from the photo of Horzt to a dozen different views of the mall's exterior. He tapped one and it blinked to life on the large bank of wall screens. Street on the south side that occasionally got car traffic. In the dull gleam of the almost-full moon's silver light, shadows bobbed and shifted. Dozens of them.

"What is that?" Astrid said.

Three more camera views came to life, all showing the streets surrounding the mall and its expansive, weedy parking lot. The bobbing shapes were all around us, keeping back but close enough for our technology to sense them.

Rufus's fingers flew over the keyboard in front of him. A heat sensor map of the immediate area showed hundreds of little red dots in a complete circle.

We were surrounded.

Astrid stalked to another computer and grabbed a microphone. The mall's intercom squealed to life. "All able-bodied human and vampire residents, report to the weapons locker. Therians, be ready to shift. We have an immediate threat outside of our perimeter. This is not a drill. Repeat. This is not a drill."

"Should we call the Coni back?" Rufus asked.

"No," Astrid replied.

I still had my blades from earlier, so I didn't wait around for the rest of the conversation, or instructions. Deep down I knew who was outside and why. I ran for the mall's entrance, not surprised to find myself flanked by a dingo and a lioness—Kyle and Lynn had joined me already. They followed me past our dozens of parked vehicles, through the magical barrier wall, and out into the cold, open air of the parking lot.

Our only entrance was at the interior curve of the U-shaped mall, and a perfect boxed canyon if we let ourselves get trapped. I jogged through the lot, all the way to the end of the mall, where it opened into a wider lot.

The night was startlingly quiet given how many creatures lurked just beyond our magical perimeter. The spell compelled humans to look away from the entire lot and made it impossible for them to directly see the building. And while we'd reinforced the underground to prevent troll attacks or access via the city's network of sewers and old bootlegger tunnels, the magic barrier was unlikely to stop a crush of goblins from swarming it at once.

Kyle loped a few feet further out, hackles raised. A low growl broke the quiet.

I palmed my blades and waited, adrenaline already coursing through me, readying me for the fight. In some ways, I'd brought this to our doorstep, but whatever went down tonight was not my fault. I never asked to be a pawn in this Fey war. I never asked to be taken by goblins and tortured to death. I never asked for any of this, and yet here I was, in the heart of it all.

Time for Nessa and her horde to finally put up or shut up.

Kismet came up beside me, decked out in chest armor and with several guns. She handed one of the armored vests to me, and I put it on. It only protected our chests and back, but considering the sharpness of goblin claws, the vest could be a lifesaver. Or at least prevent a lot of unnecessary bleeding.

More than two hundred warriors—human, Therian and vampire—fanned out across the west side of the parking lot, protecting the only way in or out of the Watchtower. Felia, Lupa, and Ursia waited in their true forms, better able to do battle that way. Smaller shifters like Sandburg wore vests and carried weapons.

Everyone wielding a gun moved to the front, ready to lay down opening fire the moment the goblins breached our perimeter.

At least a two dozen wounded, plus Rufus and the Lupa pups, were inside and in need of protection.

"Nothing gets inside the Watchtower," I shouted.

In the distance, a new sound rose. Soft at first, and indistinct, but growing in pitch. Hundreds of raspy, unpracticed voices repeating the same word over and over.

Kelsa.

Our forces shifted, restless, waiting for the horde to finally engage.

No time like the present. "You want me Nessa?" I screamed to the heavens. "Then come and fucking get me!"

I swear Kismet mentally face-palmed.

It worked, though. My tether to the Break twitched and jerked as the mass of goblins surged past our protective barrier spell. Gunfire would bring police who couldn't see what was happening in front of their faces, but bullets were our first best defense against the tide bearing down on us.

"Open fire!" I said.

The sound was deafening, a roar of bullets that joined the screams of the goblins cut down by the first volley. But they weren't only coming at us head-on. They were flanking us, too, rounding the two department stores than anchored the U, swarming from all directions. The constant barrage of bullets was creating a kind of body wall of black and fuchsia, and soon goblins began breaking through.

Hate blasted through me. Hatred for these soulless monsters who kept attacking me and the people I loved. Hatred for my job and for having to kill, over and over. Hatred for Kelsa and Nessa and any other queen who'd sent her horde to fight us tonight.

That hate warmed my belly, surged through my limbs, and jolted me into action. The first splash of goblin blood on my hands and blades fueled me to seek out another. Flesh sliced open and monsters fell. The vest protected me as much as it tried to slow me down. Canines growled. Big cats snarled. Bears roared. The ground slicked with blood and gore.

More goblins crushed their way toward us, pushing our combined forces back into the canyon. I'd never seen so many at once. It seemed as if the sewers had opened up and vomited forth every single goblin that had ever been birthed in its filth. Their sheer numbers were slowly overwhelming us.

Claws scored my thigh. I jammed a blade deep into that goblin's throat.

"Perimeter breach!" someone shouted.

I ran for the rear. A single goblin had gotten past us and was scampering toward the Watchtower entrance, seeming to know where it was despite the wall glamour. A shot rang out from somewhere inside the entrance, and the goblin's head exploded.

Good.

I couldn't see the marksman, but someone had stayed put to guard our heart.

Multiple goblins slammed into my from behind, and I face-planted on hard asphalt. Claws scraped my scalp and the back of my neck. I slashed wildly and connected with something that gave. Teeth clamped down my left hand with fiery agony. I screamed and twisted, knocking one goblin off my back while the other kept tight to my hand, ripping flesh and tendons. The third died of a gunshot, thanks to someone.

I buried my other blade in the goblin's neck, and the fucking thing let go of my hand as it died. "Mother fucker."

More clusters of goblins were breaking past our perimeter. Any that got within thirty feet of the entrance were cut down with very carefully aimed gunfire. Not a single wasted bullet, not a single stray that became friendly fire. I tucked my left hand close to my chest and took care of any stragglers with the single blade I had left.

A new sounded echoed from the distance—more gunshots. And more growling.

Someone had called in outside reinforcements.

Thank fuck.

If Nessa sent the full force of the goblin hordes at us expecting to win, she was going to get a nice big shock in the form of mass genocide. Part of me rebelled against the idea of being the cause of a species' extinction. The rest of me knew the world would be a better place without any goblins in it.

Lights flashed overhead, and I finally caught the whir of a helicopter's blades. Like they had at Olsmill so many months ago, vampire warriors dressed in black rappelled down rope lines to join the fray. A dozen new faces, somehow all packed inside a small chopper like it was a clown car.

Paul emerged from the crush of battle, his shoulders bleeding, face pasty pale. I sheathed my knife, then grabbed him around the waist with my right arm. He was still healing from some pretty bad shoulder wounds, and it looked like he'd only made them worse.

"What are you doing out here, you idiot?" I asked.

"Had to help." His head lolled a little. I dragged his ass toward the entrance, so he could get out of the way. Whoever was inside could get him to Dr. Vansis.

"You probably pulled out every stitch put into you."

"Probably."

Twenty feet from our invisible entrance, a familiar disembodied voice from inside shouted, "Duck!"

We both went to our knees, and a swish of air moved above us right where our chests were a moment earlier. I rolled Paul beneath me, angled myself up so I could see what the hell was bearing down on us.

Tall and horribly thin, like a small woman stretched out like taffy, a snarling goblin queen loomed over me. I kicked out, but she dodged my foot, crazy fast just like Kelsa had been. She was also smart enough to keep low and keep us between herself and the invisible man with the gun.

Where the hell had she come from, though?

She lashed out with a long, twisted piece of metal that looked like a giant corkscrew. I blocked her with my right forearm, and without really thinking, smashed my left hand into her throat. White fire shot up my arm from my already damaged hand. She gurgled and stumbled. I felt for my tether and it snapped tight. Pulled on my emotion tap of loneliness—not hard to find without Wyatt fighting by my side—and then pictured the open interior of the parking area.

Paul yelled, not prepared to find himself flying apart, surging through the Break, and coming back together a dozen yards away.

I rolled to my knees, my head throbbing, sick to my stomach from the pain in my hand.

"You two with me?"

I turned toward the voice and nearly fell over. Rufus was dead center in the entrance, wheelchair locked, with a sniper rifle in his hands. He was the one who'd spoken, but he wasn't alone. To the left, using the wall for support, Milo stood with another rifle tucked up against his shoulder.

"She came down the wall," Milo said. "Bitch must have climbed up and over while we were distracted out front."

Wow. A goblin with a tactical plan. Who knew?

"Stay here," I said to Paul as I stood on shaky legs.

He gave me a thumbs up.

I stumbled over to Rufus and peered out. Nessa was gone. "What the hell? Are female goblins closeted rock climbers, or something?"

"No idea," Rufus said. "But she was up the mall wall the moment you teleported."

"Great."

The fight was still going strong near the mouth of the U, with fewer goblins escaping our line of defense. Milo and Rufus took turns picking them off. I waited with them, refusing to go with Dr. Vansis when he came to collect Paul. My mostly useless left hand meant I was more of a liability out there now, but I hated doing nothing while others fought.

Until Alejandro broke from the line, limping and bleeding from half a dozen places. He inched along the mall wall, no weapons on him that I could see. The kid was young and needed way more field training, but I had to give him a gold star for trying. He also had a long way to go to get back here for medical treatment.

Without thinking, I found my tether and slipped into the Break. The second teleport left me crazy dizzy, but I grabbed him and said, "Hold on tight."

His surprised yelp faded as we both teleported back into the garage. I caught him as he fell, alarmed at all of the bleeding wounds on his neck and legs. My stomach threatened to up-end, but I applied pressure as best I could.

"What did we do?" he asked.

"Magic." He was fading. "Hold on, kiddo, help is on the way."

"Wanted to help."

"Yeah? How many did you kill?"

His lips quirked. "Not enough."

I smiled. "Good answer."

Footsteps thundered down the corridor toward us. I looked up, expecting Dr. Vansis, and instead saw Mark and Peter running toward me.

"What are you doing here?" I snapped.

"We want to help," Peter said. "Please, we can help."

I did not want those pups anywhere near the fighting. "Fine, carry Alejandro here to the infirmary."

They jumped to action. Peter grabbed Alejandro around the shoulders, while Mark grabbed his thighs. Despite their wiry frames, the boys were strong, and they moved fast.

"And here I didn't think anything else could surprise me today," I said, mostly to myself.

"Bite your tongue," Milo snapped.

I stood, shaky and woozy, and boy howdy my head wanted to explode, but Nessa was still out there. This wasn't over yet. I palmed my blade again and stumbled closer to the open entrance, half-expecting Nessa to drop down in the center of it at any moment.

More of our wounded began to break away from the fighting.

"Don't even think about it," Rufus said. "You're one person, Stone. You can't teleport them all."

I glared at him.

"Use a van," Milo said. "It's a hundred feet. Drive them back."

"I don't have a license." Okay, as far as stupid, pain-brain things to say, that was a good one. "And one-handed?"

"Good point."

Somehow I missed the return of the pups, because Peter said, "I can drive."

"No way," I said.

"Please." Peter went down to one knee like someone about to propose—or someone about to plead to his Alpha. "Let us help your people. It's the least we can do for all you've done for us."

I frowned. "If you get hurt, Wyatt's going to kill me. Not literally, but just…don't get hurt."

"We won't."

All of the vehicles had keys in them for easy access. Peter and Mark chose one of our utility vans, while Rufus moved his chair out of the way. Peter drove them out in the roar of a gunning engine and the sour smell of exhaust. He aimed for what looked like the far wall, then executed a perfect turn that ended in a tire-squealing stop by our three wounded.

I couldn't see for the van blocking the view, but I counted to less than ten before the van headed back our way. Peter drove right past us and down the corridor, hand-delivering them to the infirmary.

Wyatt would have been so fucking proud.

Will be.

The pups were out on their third run, van barreling back toward us, when I realized our mistake all along. Too late, Nessa dropped onto the roof of the van an instant before it crossed the glamour. She launched herself at me, and the impact had us both rolling across the cement floor.

We slammed into the side of a car. Before I could orient myself, Nessa shoved me onto my back and arched down with that corkscrew knife. I blocked with my right arm but not fast enough. The blade pierced my vest and sank into the skin beneath. Right over my heart. I used my screaming left for support as she bore down. My arms burned with the effort of keeping her at bay. Preventing her from plunging that awful, twisted knife into my heart. She wasn't bigger than me, but my mangled left hand and too many teleports gave her the advantage.

"Be careful, Milo."

"I can't get a clean shot."

"Shoot her anyway!" I yelled, because in about five seconds that curly knife was going into my chest. It dug in another centimeter, blossoming blood and more pain from the wound.

A shadow moved behind her. Nessa slashed out with one hand, releasing some pressure from the blade. Milo screamed, and something thudded. I tried to roll, but Nessa still had me pinned. She hurled her weight at me and the knife, and it went deeper.

I couldn't heal from a direct stabbing of the heart.

Wyatt. I'm sorry.

A flash of a furry gray coat was my only warning before strong jaws clamped down on the back of Nessa's neck and shook her. Nessa screeched. Her mission to impale me was forgotten by her sudden need to slash at the canine that was hauling her away. I yanked the blade out of my chest and sat up.

One of the Lupa pups slammed Nessa's face into the concrete. Bone cracked. She went limp enough for the pup to sit down on her body, jaws still firmly clamped around her neck. Behind them, Milo was holding a bleeding arm close to his chest.

"Stone?" Rufus.

"We're alive," I said. I'd rolled behind a row of cars, and if he'd stayed to play sniper, he had no idea. "Nessa's in a choke hold. Milo?"

He winced. "I'll live. You?"

"Same." I really didn't want to think about how close a shave that had been. I scooted closer to the pup who had to be Mark. I'd only seen the three in their true forms once, and Mark and John were nearly identical. Mark must have jumped from the van and raced back to help. "You want to do some heavy lifting?"

The pup blinked hard, so I took that as a yes.

I somehow got back on my feet. Milo waved me off helping him, so I limped back to the entrance. The pup followed, dragging Nessa along with him, leaving a streak of fuchsia in their wake. She wasn't dead, but she also wasn't struggling when one sharp turn could snap her neck.

At the end of the U, the battle seemed to be turning in our favor. We took Nessa halfway.

"Raise her up so they can see her face," I said.

He did, using his strong true form to practically hold her upright. She hissed at me, blood streaking her face from her crushed nose. I gripped the twisted knife in my hand and pressed the tip to the soft flesh beneath her chin.

"Nessa is beaten!" I shouted. My voice bounced off the walls, gaining the attention of both goblins and my people. And instead of rushing me, the goblins stopped moving completely. As if unable to compute the sight of their queen at the mercy of a human female. When enough goblin eyeballs were on me, I shoved the blade into Nessa's neck.

She gurgled as she died.

Mournful wails rose up, and our side took complete advantage. More goblins were cut down, but that part of the fight was no longer my problem. I released the knife handle.

"Let her go," I said.

The pup did, and her body splatted to the ground. He moved to my side and licked my right hand. I stroked the soft fur around his muzzle. "Thank you."

I swear he smiled.

"Holy shit, dude." Mark's voice behind me startled me into turning around.

Mark and Peter were staring at us both, open-mouthed, not even hiding their disbelief. Or their pride. I glanced down at the Lupa by my side, shock turning into respect for his bravery.

John had saved my life.

"You did good, kiddo," I said.

He wagged his big tail.

"So did you two," I said to Mark and Peter. "Thank you for helping with the wounded."

"You're welcome," Peter said. "They attacked our home. We needed to do something."

"You did. All three of you did."

I looked at Nessa's corpse, and then past her to the rising pile of goblin remains. Sirens wailed in the distance. The fight was over, and the cleanup would be horrendous, but the police wouldn't be able to see anything. Our troops were exhausted and ragged, and many were wounded, and tonight was only the first battle.

In only a few more hours we'd throw down the gauntlet in the final war to be waged with the Fey.

I just hoped we were ready.

CHAPTER TEN

01:20

Distant conversations made excellent background noise for my attempts to Zen out and ignore the constant itch-ache in my left hand as it healed. After allowing Dr. Vansis to poke a few things into place, he wrapped the hand, and I retreated to the recreation room to wait for my gnome gift to kick in. Now that it had, it was driving me nuts. Even with my eyes closed, I couldn't focus on anything else.

Apparently I'd come pretty close to permanent, not-healable ligament damage.

Yay me.

The heap of goblin corpses were being disposed of by our able-bodied personnel, as well as extra help sent in by several of the Clan Elders. Rufus had called them for assistance the moment he realized how many goblins we were facing, and the opposing forces coming in from the outside had helped create a boxed canyon of our own for the goblins. Made them a lot easier to kill.

Somehow our side had come through with no fatalities. A few series injuries, both human and Therian, and a ton of flesh wounds. I think one vampire mussed their hair.

Itch-throb-ache. Itch-throb-ache.

The hand would heal in a day or two, but goddamn the ability was annoying sometimes. Especially with serious wounds. If we didn't have a Fey war looming at dawn, I'd have asked Dr. Vansis for some nice drugs to ease me through it.

All around me, clusters of less-than-able-bodied people were talking, moving around, probably wondering about our next step. One pair of shuffling footsteps stopped near my couch. I slitted an eyelid to take a peek.

Kismet stared down at me, a bandage on her right shoulder the only immediately sign of damage. "Looks like we finally solved your goblin problem."

"I hope so." The last thing I needed was yet another goblin queen deciding to exact revenge for Kelsa and Nessa.

"Wyatt's going to be pissed when he finds out the Lupa helped."

"Tell me something I don't know." I fully opened both eyes. Kismet glanced at the couch. I raised my knees so she could sit near my feet, but I stayed flat on my back. "On the plus side, none of them were injured."

"True." She grunted. "I could kill Milo for being anywhere near that fight in his state."

"It's instinct to do something to help. At least he stayed inside."

"Marcus is going to shit himself when he sees those claw marks, though."

I couldn't help a small gust of laughter. "Is Phineas going to shit himself when he sees your claw marks?"

"What?"

Her what had been way too careful. I dragged my tired ass up into a sitting position and tucked one knee under me. She stared at me with practiced confusion. "Oh come on, Gina. How long have you and Phin been"—I made air quotes with one hand—"seeing each other?"

"We're not seeing each other."

"So you're just fucking?"

She glared. Answer enough.

"How long?" I asked, genuinely curious. And not in an I'm-jealous way, because I'd never felt that for Phineas, and God knew Kismet deserved someone amazing like him. "Since he came back with Brevin? Before he left?"

"Look, we're both adults with needs, and we have good sex. Can you drop it now?"

"If it's just casual sex, then how come Phin was so closed-lip when I asked him earlier?"

Her glare softened. "Maybe he likes his privacy, too."

"Look at us, you and me and Milo finally getting personal lives, and we all fall for big Alpha types who have to go risk their lives to save the world."

Kismet groaned. "I liked you better when I was trying to kill you."

I blew her a kiss.

"Seriously, though," she said. "The goblin fight was a nice distraction, but all of this waiting around for sunrise is driving me crazy."

"I know what you mean. Being so far away from the epicenter of the fight is not what I'm used to."

"You're used to being smack in the middle of it."

"Exactly." I scratched at a patch of skin above my elbow that wasn't covered in bandages, desperate to get at the part of my arm that really fucking itched. "I also really hate not knowing what to anticipate from Amalie. Goblins attack a threat. Halfies attack a threat. The Fey? They send others in to fight, or try to swoop in sideways via manipulation."

Kismet nodded. "We've never battled the Fey, so we have no way to anticipate their move once the Tainted are summoned."

"Bingo. I mean, yeah, if Brevin's plan works, we'll have three super soldiers on our side to help wipe the mat with them, but where? And when?"

"The fact that time moves differently for the Fey is both a blessing and a curse."

Therein lay the heart of our problem with anticipating and planning. We were counting on Amalie's inattention so we could get the Tainted into our hosts. But that same inattention might mean hours or even days before they reacted. And the longer our loved ones held the Tainted, the smaller their chances of survival became.

"Did Wyatt ever tell you that the first time we laid eyes on each other was in a cemetery?" Kismet said.

Talk about apropos of nothing.

"No, he didn't." I sat a little straighter, intrigued by the random tidbit of personal information. "Wyatt doesn't like talking about the past. A cemetery seems fitting, though."

She smiled. "It was my first day back in the city after my dishonorable Army discharge."

"Dishonorable? When do I get that story?"

"Maybe after the apocalypse is over. Anyway, I came back the day of a good friend's funeral, and afterward, as I was walking away, I spotted him standing by a pair of headstones."

"His parents and brother?"

"Yes. It was only a few days after Nicandro died, and I was struck by his sadness. He looked up at me, and our eyes met. Somehow I knew deep down that I'd see him again, even though we didn't say a word to each other."

"When did you find out what Wyatt did for a living?"

"About a year later. I got wasted at a nightclub and went into the back alley to have sex with the guy I was with. Turns out he was a Halfie looking for a snack. Wyatt saved my life. Not long after, he recruited me into the earliest version of what became the Triads."

An early version that included Rufus. The secret he'd told me—the huge thing I'd kept from Wyatt for months now—tickled my brain. "Gina, back then did Wyatt ever talk about the bounty hunters who killed his family?"

"Not much. I know he still wants to find the one that got away, but I think he's accepted he probably never will. Not after so much time." Never one to miss a detail, Kismet's eyebrows dipped. "Why?"

I really, really wanted to get this thing off my chest, and Kismet hadn't betrayed me in months—not since we both realized we made better allies than enemies. "I know who the bounty hunter is."

Her entire body jerked. "You what? Who? How have you not told him yet?"

"Because it's someone Wyatt knows and trusts, and even though they didn't swear me to not tell, I...I don't know. We've all lost so much these last six months. I didn't want Wyatt to lose another friend."

"Friend." She blinked several times as understanding settled in. "Holy shit, it's one of us. Someone who was folded into the Watchtower from the Triads?"

I nodded, unable to speak against the lump in my throat.

"You're protecting them because you know Wyatt's temper," Kismet said.

"I don't want to be the one who blows apart their friendship. Not after everything they've been through."

"Fuck me." Her face went slack. "Rufus?"

I looked at my lap, which was all the confirmation she needed.

"I'll be damned," she said, a little breathless. "Well, that explains why Rufus was such an asshole to Wyatt at the start of things."

"Yeah." I glanced around but no one seemed to be paying attention. I lowered my voice anyhow, because Therian ears were in the room. "Rufus told me once he felt sick about what happened at the diner. That he was working with an older bounty hunter and basically did as told. He joined the early Triads as a way to pay for what he'd done, and that he didn't want to be Wyatt's friend because of what he'd taken from him."

"But they ended up friends anyway."

"Yeah, they did. And I know Wyatt. He swore a long time ago that he'd find and punish both men who killed his family."

"You're afraid if you tell him, he'll try to kill Rufus."

"I know he will. He'll try, others will step in to stop it, and it will be a huge mess. And then he'll be super-pissed at me for keeping the secret in the first place, even though it's technically not my secret to tell."

"Then don't tell it." Kismet's sharp statement got my complete attention. "Maybe Rufus was trying to clear his conscience by telling you, I don't know, but he shouldn't have. He should not have burdened you with this, even if he'd hoped you would save him the trouble of confessing by telling Wyatt yourself. This is his problem to fix, not yours. If Rufus wants atonement, he has to ask for it."

I turned her words over in my mind, finding a lot of sense in them. Rufus had confessed during a dark time in his life—wounded, no prospects for the future, before the Watchtower was created and he accepted an offer to work here. Maybe he'd wanted me to tell Wyatt so Wyatt would put Rufus out of his misery.

But I hadn't wanted that. Rufus was a friend and a vital part of Operations. Kismet was right. If he wanted to be absolved, he needed to fess up on his own.

"Thanks," I said. "For putting some perspective on that."

"No problem."

"How much longer until sunrise?"

She checked her phone. "A little over an hour."

My tether to the Break sputtered and sparkled. Magic was happening somewhere, and in strong doses. Were the elves starting the procedure early, or was something else going down?

"Stone?"

I shook out my entire body. "Break hiccup. I'm not sure what that was about." And I knew, way deep down in my bones, it was only a matter of time before I found out.

Whatever's happening out there, Wyatt, please take care of yourself.

Come back to me.

CHAPTER ELEVEN

00:16

My plan to spend the next half hour or so stalking Ops for news on what was happening in the mountains was put on hold by a strange text from Milo: *My room. NOW*.

I shot back that I was on my way—texting with only my right hand was definitely being added to my least favorite methods of communicating—then started hoofing it. I ignored curious looks from folks who probably expected me to be heading in the exact opposite direction. The dorms were mostly empty, except for the wounded who required sleep.

Milo's door was half-open. He was sitting on the floor facing his bed, which had a laptop open on it, ear buds in. I clapped my hands to get his attention. He yanked the earbuds out as he half-closed the laptop.

"If you called me here to watch a cat video on YouTube," I said, "I'm going to strangle you."

"Can you keep a secret?" he asked.

Interesting.

"Remember who you're talking to?" I plunked down next to him. "Is this you sharing your addiction to online porn?"

He snorted, some of the stress easing from his face. "Be serious for a sec, okay?"

"Really? The men we love are about to become the outer wrapping of a demon burrito, and you want me to stop being sarcastic? You do realize that would mean running around screaming at people in fear and frustration, right?"

All I got for that was a long, slow blink.

"Okay, fine," I said. "What's up?"

"Marcus went in bugged."

For the briefest moment, I thought that was some kind of innuendo. And then it struck me. "Into the cave? He's wired?"

"Yes." Milo lifted the laptop screen. The image made my heart flutter.

Angled low, like the bug was on the floor, it had a good view of the interior of the earthen room I remembered so well. Instead of six large crates housing hell-beasts, the room was empty except for six people. Directly ahead was Phineas, with Brevin to his left. On the right side of the screen, at an angle, stood Wyatt and the third elf I didn't know. Marcus and Sorvin were barely visible on the left side of the screen. In the center of them all was the pool of rippling black water.

The fact that our guys were standing around in their boxers surprised me more than it should. When Tovin was possessed by the Tainted, it had warped his body. Made him grow bigger and taller. Uglier.

An impending Hulk-out made the shorts pretty reasonable.

"Marcus put the bug in his belt buckle," Milo said. "The elves didn't want technology in the cave, but Marcus wanted eyes down there. Just in case."

"Sneaky little kitty cat, isn't he?"

He handed me one of the ear buds. I tucked it in, but the only thing I could hear was very low chanting in a weird language.

"They've been doing this for, like, an hour," Milo said.

"You've been watching for an hour and you just now told me?" I resisted the urge to smack him upside the head. He'd been hurt enough today, and the thick bandage on his left arm was still stained red. "How's your arm?"

"Hurts like a mother fucker. You?"

"Itches like a mother fucker." I stared at Wyatt, but the distance kept me from seeing the nuances that would tell me more about his thoughts. He stood at attention, like Phineas, but almost seemed…bored.

I'd be bored too if I'd been standing around for an hour listening to elves chanting.

Outside the sky was likely turning from black to navy, with the first hints of real light in the east. Sunrise was soon. Something would finally be happening *soon*.

My tether to the Break lashed and sparked, alerting me to the shift in magic. Onscreen, the rippling black pool began to swirl, faster and faster. I could only see the motion of the water, but I could imagine the vortex forming in the center—the same thing I'd witnessed when Tovin summoned his Tainted. The noise and energy in the air had to be breathtaking, if the sounds in my earbud were any indication.

His gaze was fixed on the whirlpool, but I didn't miss the tremor that ran through Wyatt's body—fear or adrenaline, or maybe a mix of both. The elves' collective voices rose in pitch, speaking in another language.

I didn't realize I'd grabbed Milo's hand until the force of his squeezing mine made a bone creak. My tether came alive, urging me to use it. To teleport. To become part of the Break. I resisted hard, trying to focus on the screen in front of me. Needing to see this.

One elf voice rose higher than the rest, and it took me a sec to track it to Brevin. Up from the pool floated a shapeless black blob, shimmery and ghostlike, about the size of a house cat. It floated toward Brevin.

Toward Phineas.

My heart twisted tight. Bile scorched the back of my throat.

Brevin spoke. Phineas took a step forward, shoulders back, head held high, seeming to stare the black mass down.

I touched the screen by his face, hating that I wasn't there to help. To show my friend I loved him, would always love him, and would always have his back.

Time seemed to stop for an instant—and then the Tainted slid forward, plastered itself against Phineas's bare chest like some kind of paint splatter, and disappeared.

Phineas released a pained roar unlike anything I'd ever heard from man or beast. Hands clutching at his chest, he fell to his knees, alternately panting and groaning. His majestic wings sprouted from his shoulder blades, the once beautiful brown and white mottling now a dusky gray. Gray that darkened to pitch black leather as his body began to swell.

Bare skin darkened to a horrific shade of violet like the worst kind of bruise. His entire body mass seemed to increased at least twenty percent in both height and muscles. The pained sounds stopped. He shook out both hands, head still ducked low, and I swore I spotted black claws on his fingers.

"Jesus," Milo said.

Then Phineas raised his head, and I nearly pissed myself. Gone was the stunningly handsome friend I'd known. His blue eyes had turned black, empty. Violet skin was oily and slick looking, and his jaw jutted out too far. His nose too long and sharp.

Marcus hissed.

Phineas snapped his head to the side, probably looking at Marcus. Assessing him.

What if the elf can't control the Tainted? What if Phin goes nuts and kills Marcus?

Brevin said a word that sounded a lot like "bearded tree." Phineas looked down at him, his entire body rippling with energy. And then he knelt.

He fucking knelt on one knee like a dude about to propose.

"Holy shit," I said. "Did it work? Does this mean it worked?"

"I think so."

One down, two to go.

Sorvin went next, and I curled both of my hands around Milo's while we watched Marcus go through the same bone-chilling transformation. Same increase size, same shiny bruised skin. We couldn't see enough of Marcus's face to know how that had changed, but in the end, Sorvin said "bearded tree," or whatever, and Marcus knelt too.

I cast around for something to throw up in. Wyatt was next.

With our attention on Marcus, I hadn't seen Wyatt bi-shift into his half-Lupa form. Probably to help him accept the Tainted more easily, but goddamn, I hated that I'd missed one last look at his handsome face.

It won't be your last. Stop it.

The third elf spoke the same words as the previous two, and a third black blob floated up out of the swirling pool. My tether pulled at me, demanding I use it. My love for Wyatt told me to take hold of that need and go to him. Only Milo's tight grip kept me still, rooted to the concrete floor, while a demon latched onto my lover's chest and disappeared.

I couldn't stop the sob that ripped from my throat.

Four and a half years of our entwined lives flashed through my mind like a manic highlights reel: the first whiskey toast at my introduction to Jesse and Ash; my first in-field Halfie kill, down by the Corcoran train bridge; the first time Wyatt said "suck it up, buttercup" after I complained about patrolling with a sprained wrist; him nursing me through the flu this past spring; his face as I lay dying on that stained mattress in the abandoned train station.

The first time he told me he loved me.

The first time we made love.

The last time we made love.

I watched the man I loved more than myself shift and change into a monster I barely recognized. His face became more wolf-like, with sharp teeth and gleaming black eyes. Claws on his fingers. On his toes. Purple skin so wrong that I wanted to scream.

He shook himself out, then snarled in Phineas's direction.

His assigned elf said the magic kneeling words.

Wyatt snarled a second time.

Uh oh.

The elf said, "Bearded tree skirt!" Or something. I didn't have an elf-to-English translator on hand.

Wyatt's head snapped in the elf's direction, his face a twisted mask of anger and hate. "How dare you?" he said in a voice from the pit of Hell. So deep and sickeningly inhuman.

"We offer you vengeance," said all three elves in unison, like some awful Greek chorus. "We offer a chance for you to punish those who have wronged you."

"Your kind saw us banished, and yet you have imprisoned us here in these vessels. You are fools."

"This world is no longer for our kind. The sprites wish to see it cleansed of humankind, the very creatures that so attract you here."

Wyatt tilted his head, clearly listening to the elf chorus. "Humankind has such delicious emotions. This world pulses with them."

"Amalie would see that pulse stopped. Permanently."

"No."

I glanced at Milo, whose wide eyes found mine. I had no idea what to expect once the Tainted were across the Break, but this was going way more peacefully than I'd anticipated. The first Tainted had been righteously pissed off and ready to do some serious damage to the world—and to my freshly resurrected body.

These three were actually…well, calm. Calculating.

Brevin and his brothers had done something a hell of a lot better than Tovin's original summoning, because these Tainted seemed to be under control.

For now.

"Help us defeat the Fey seeking to destroy humankind," the chorus said.

"For what reward?" Wyatt asked.

Uh oh. They probably won't do tricks for a handshake and a sincere thank you.

"Information," was the reply. "One of your brethren was summoned to this world many months ago. We know where he is. Assist us, return to your realm willingly, and your brother will be returned to you."

"The fuck he will," I snapped at the computer.

Those asshole elves had no right to bargain with our contained Tainted.

Only Wyatt seemed to be considering it. "If he is truly here and not destroyed, why can I not sense him?"

"He is being contained by magic."

Milo let out a sharp breath. "This is insane. The Tainted is actually considering helping us fight a war go get another of his kind back?"

"We've done that and worse to save our friends," I replied. "Amalie told me that the Tainted are all emotion and instinct, unable to make moral decisions." Then again, everything Amalie ever told me was suspect. "But maybe they make attachments like we do. I mean, they've been together for, like, a million years or something."

"I wonder if Gina or Astrid know the elves are bargaining with our Tainted."

"No idea." The elves had been playing this part of the plan very tight and for good reason. Giving back the trapped Tainted was a huge play, and not one many of us would have backed.

"Father," Marcus said, his hellish voice startling. "It is a chance for mayhem unlike anything we have tasted in millennia. And Darash is my husband."

Milo squeaked.

If I wasn't already sitting, I'd have probably fallen over. Not only did the Tainted who tried to kill me had a name after all, but Marcus was hosting a female demon.

I cannot wait to tease him about this.

In the distance, Phineas seemed bored by the entire thing.

"We agree to your bargain," Wyatt said. "We are in your service to stop the eradication of humankind, in exchange for the return of our brethren."

"Agreed," said the three-elf chorus.

Something squealed—a familiar noise, like a door opening. I glanced behind me, like an idiot, but it was the door to the cave. The three Tainted men looked past the direction of our camera, while the elves remained with their heads tilted down. Still concentrating on containing the Tainted.

I waited for the newcomer to move into view, but they didn't. "Accompany me to the surface," a male voice said. Took me a minute to recognize Pike's voice.

"Go," the three elves said. "The Coni will guide you."

Everything inside of me screamed out against the idea of the clutch of Coni warriors being exposed to three Tainted. I didn't trust the Tainted, not even with the amazing amount of restraint and control they were showing, thanks to their hosts.

Wyatt went first, Marcus last, until only the elves remained in their triangle around the pool. The chanting resumed.

"Well fuck," I said with a grunt. "Guess the show's over for now."

Milo flopped onto his back and let out a long sigh. "That sucked. Really, really sucked."

"Yeah, it did. But they got through it."

"So far." Splayed out like that with a bandage on his arm made Milo look so young. Not innocent. But young. Twenty years old and so much life left to live.

"After this I'm done." The words slipped without thought or reason, because they were the truth.

His head listed to the side, eyes scrunched. "Done with what?"

"All of this. Me and Wyatt and the boys? We're leaving the city. We're both ready to start a new life without all of the violence and bloodshed."

He sat up slowly, wounded arm cradled in his lap. "Wanting it and actually doing it are two different things, Evy. Can you really leave this behind? The Watchtower and everything we're doing to protect the city?"

"Yes, I can." I ran fingers through my hair, unsurprised when bits of dried blood flaked out. I was holding off on a shower until my arm finished healing. "My entire life, I've felt unwanted. My mother didn't want me, foster families didn't want me. When the state kicked me out at eighteen, I was facing jail or the Triads, and if I had to make the choice again? I'd probably choose jail."

I held up a hand because I saw the argument coming. "And yes, I know that means I'd have never met Wyatt, and I'd have never made the friendships that I have, but I also wouldn't be living with this giant ball of guilt in my heart. Everything that has happened since my first death has somehow revolved around me. Every person who has died? Baylor, Jenner, Felix, Tybalt. Hell, the entire Coni and Stri Clan. I'm tangentially responsible for their deaths, and it fucking sucks. I don't want my presence here to cause any more deaths, and neither does Wyatt.

"For almost five years, my entire life has been about killing. I had something to fight for. To die for. But Milo, for the first time in my life I have something to live for. Really live for. To be at peace for."

Milo blinked hard several times, and I swore I saw moisture on his eyelashes. "Who are you?" he said with a smile. "And what have you done with Evy Stone?"

I laughed, and it felt good. "She fell in love and finally grew up."

"It only took dying how many times?"

"Technically only twice. Demetrius slicing me open with a sword didn't actually make my heart stop." It had hurt like a motherfucker, though, especially when that shit started to heal. Faking my death so a revenge-bent werecat didn't slaughter my kind-of-parents had seemed like a good idea at the time. Pissed off a lot of people, though, and my "dying" had been the reason Aurora, Ava, and Joseph fled the city.

Aurora was back though, and damn it, I wanted to know what was going on in the mountains.

"Do you think Amalie knows you're still alive?" Milo asked.

The abrupt conversation switch had me backpedaling fast. "Huh?"

"You said once that Amalie could sense you and Wyatt in the city, because you'd both been in the presence of her true form. But when Thackery had you, your heart stopped once. You died a second time. Do you think that death broke her connection to you?"

I blinked at him. "I have no idea. We haven't had any contact with the Fey since the attack on Boot Camp this summer."

Wyatt said once, when the last of the Triads were told about the idea of the Watchtower, that I had been the wild card Amalie never saw coming. I confounded her, making choices she hadn't anticipated and ruining her plans all over the place. If she couldn't sense me anymore, maybe I could be that wild card again.

But how could we use that to our advantage when we had no idea how or when the Fey would engage?

They couldn't have possibly missed the huge surge in power from the Break during the three summonings. Someone was going to investigate. Hell, the location of our troops wasn't all that far from First Break. All Amalie had to do was send a pixie to the surface to scout for her, and they'd find a few dozen Coni warriors ready to throw down.

My phone chimed with a text. 911 to Ops.

"Something's happening," I said.

"Figured." Milo grunted as I helped him stand. "I hate that I can't go with you."

"I know." I hugged him, then planted a kiss on his forehead. "But I like knowing at least one of my friends is safe and sound during the end of the world."

He pulled a face. "Still. Be safe, okay?"

"I will. And I'll do my best to bring our guys home in one piece."

"Okay."

I winked as I left, hoping it made the entire thing more tolerable. Milo was a warrior, same as me. He wanted to help save lives, and all he could do was remain behind and heal from old wounds. Part of me wished that Thackery had been able to find something physical about my healing ability—something he could have reproduced to help others heal faster. But he hadn't, because it was a gnome gift. Magic.

The only thing that would help Milo heal was time.

Every able-bodied person in the place had, apparently, also been summoned to Ops. A crowd had formed in the corridor outside, full of familiar faces. Mark, John and Peter stood near the wall, a bit apart from the crowd, shadowed by Quince and Eulan. I joined them, pleased to see Quince back at the Watchtower. I'd managed one operation with him before the vampire virus forced all of our allies, sick or not, to be sequestered. He hadn't been infected like so many others, and he stood tall and strong.

Ready to fight again.

The pups all seemed nervous, probably ready for a scolding for even being there, but I didn't say a word. We were all waiting to know what was happening, and they had as much riding on Wyatt's safety as I did. They were his blood now.

A commotion near the Ops doorway had heads turning. Astrid appeared to tower over everyone, probably standing on a chair, and the crowd went silent.

"We've received word that the three Tainted have successfully been summoned and contained within our volunteers," Astrid said.

That's the big news?

Oh, yeah. Milo and I had cheated.

Murmurs rippled around the large group of people. Humans, Therians, vampires, all coming together for one purpose—defeating the Fey. Saving our world.

"Nevada reports no unusual activity in or around the forest," Astrid continued. "Our teams on patrol also report very little activity since the goblin attack earlier this evening. We're going to mobilize four more teams in the next ten minutes so there are people in the field for faster response in case someone does decide to start something. Rufus will send out the assignments in a few."

"So what about the rest of us?" someone from the crowd asked. "What now?"

Astrid pinned them with a fierce glare. "Now we wait."

I suppressed a groan. I hated waiting. I'd been waiting all fucking night.

She jumped down from her chair, effectively ending the announcement.

"We want to help," Peter said.

"I know you do." I nearly reached out and ruffled his hair, which was a weirdly affectionate impulse. "You boys helped so much earlier this morning."

"We can do more."

"Well, none of you are going out into the field. Wyatt would skin me if I let you do that. None of you have any sort of proper training." My brain spun off on ways to get these three into fighting shape, with proper self-defense skills, and I had to shut that down. No more fighting after this. Not for the pups, and not for me and Wyatt. "Look, if you boys want to help, go see if Dr. Vansis needs assistance with the wounded. You can bring them food and water, if nothing else."

"I like Dr. Vansis," John said. "He doesn't treat us like we're monsters."

"That's because you aren't monsters. Thackery raised you to believe some pretty awful things, but that doesn't mean you have to continue living with hate in your hearts. Or that we should keep blaming you for actions taken during a time of extreme emotional duress."

My heart twisted sharply as I realized how much I'd come to care for these three teenage boys, and for what I'd taken from them. "I'm so sorry about your brothers," I said.

Mark and John shared a sad look.

Peter scowled. "We participated in the kidnappings and murders of your friends, Evangeline. You don't owe us apologies. Not after taking us in and giving us a second chance."

I did owe them. I'd stood there and watched two of their brothers—fucking teenagers—tortured for information, and then ultimately executed. It hadn't felt right at the time, and it felt even worse with the distance of time. Knowing they'd been raised and brainwashed by a madman.

"I'm still sorry," I said.

"If you could forgive us for what we did," John said, "then we forgive you, in return."

"Done."

John smiled, and I couldn't help myself. I slung an arm around his shoulders in a sideways hug.

My favorite red-headed cohort sidled up to us. "I'm heading out on a patrol team," Kismet said, her face set, a warrior ready for battle. "I'll see you out there somewhere, yeah?"

I nodded. "See you out there. Watch your six, okay?"

"Always."

Kismet disappeared into the crowd. My phone hadn't beeped with a message, which didn't completely surprise me. My left hand still wasn't fully functional, so I wouldn't do a patrol team a lot of good. I definitely knew how Milo felt about being left behind.

And then my phone did beep. Only it wasn't about a patrol, it was a text from Astrid telling me to get my ass into the War Room, ASAP.

"You three go make yourself useful in the infirmary," I said to the pups. "I have somewhere to be."

"Be safe, Evangeline," John said.

"I'll do my best."

Rufus nodded at me from his terminal as I passed him, and I nodded back. The War Room held several people I did not expect to see there. Eulan and Isleen sat together, across the table from Elder Rojay of Cania and Elder Dane of Felia. Two of the youngest Elders in the Clan Assembly, they had both been the staunchest, fiercest supporters of the Watchtower since its inception. Plus Eulan and Isleen were vampire royalty.

I was a little out of my league, and yet every person in that room looked at me with respect. Even Astrid.

The next thing that caught my attention was the screen on the wall and the feature film playing out. Coni warriors standing in lines, waiting. The image was a little shaky, like a hand-cam. I nearly laughed when I realized Astrid had done exactly what Marcus did.

"Who's wearing the bug?" I asked as I settled into a chair near Isleen.

"Aurora agreed to wear it," Astrid replied. "I wasn't about to send my brother out there without being able to watch what's happening."

"Smart move. Can you talk to her?"

"Of course." Astrid hit a button on the screen control, and a dim murmur filled the room. Low voices. Distant growls. "Stone's with us now."

"Good to know." Aurora's disembodied voice crackled over the sound system. "Have you prepared her?"

"Not yet."

Prepared me for what?

"The Tainted changed them, Stone," Astrid said. "Really changed them."

"I expected it to," I replied. "I've seen what the Tainted can do to an elf, so I can imagine what it would do to a Therian."

"It may be worse than you imagine. Aurora."

The camera angle changed, centering on my three Tainted allies. Seeing them again in the brightening light of dawn only heightened the otherness of their appearances, and it made their purple skin seem to ripple. As if water moved below the surface. Water as inky as what was in that pool.

I did my best to look horrified but I'd never been a very good actress.

Astrid groaned. "You've already seen them like this, haven't you?"

"Can I plead the fifth on that?"

"How the hell—no, never mind. I don't want to know."

Aurora made a sound not quite like laughter. "You never cease to surprise me, Evangeline."

"I didn't mastermind this one, if it helps," I said. "So this is us? Hanging out until something interesting happens?"

"Pretty much," Astrid said.

"If I had know there would be a movie, I would have brought popcorn."

That actually got a small smile from Isleen.

"Astrid told us of how the Lupa you protect helped save lives today," Elder Rojay said.

I sat a bit straighter. The Assembly had been torn about allowing the pups to live, much less live in the heart of the Watchtower, but Wyatt and I had both been prepared to throw down to protect them. Their continued existence was due in no small part to me and Wyatt volunteering ourselves to be held accountable if they went rogue and hurt someone.

Instead, they'd defied expectations and done some good.

"They did," I said. "Without being asked or prompted, they volunteered themselves. One of them saved my life during my fight with Nessa."

Elder Rojay tilted his head to the side. "Then they have earned our gratitude."

"Awesome. Does that mean a permanent stay of execution?"

"Stone," Astrid snapped. She didn't like me getting lippy with Clan Elders.

Rojay smiled. "That is not my sole call to make but their contribution will be addressed at our next Assembly."

Oh goodie.

Nothing remotely interesting happened for close to an hour. The Coni on screen seemed as restless as those of us watching from the War Room. Even the three Tainted grew agitated, and that wasn't a good sign. We'd brought them over to *do something*, not stand around in silence and stare at the woods.

No one was more relieved than me when the intercom buzzed.

Astrid hit the button. "Dane."

"It's Jackson." His deep voice bellowed through the speakers. "There's a police car on Cherrydale road, heading toward the Olsmill cut-off. We just turned on to follow it."

"How close to the cut-off?" Astrid asked.

"Half a mile and closing in."

"If they turn, you intercept immediately."

"Understood."

A police patrol stumbling across several dozen bi-shifted Coni and three very scary looking humanoid-demon thingies could put a serious dent in today's plan.

"They're turning," Jackson said. "Intercepting now."

"Aurora, are you copying this?" Astrid asked.

"Yes," she replied immediately.

"Hold tight until we know what we're dealing with."

"Acknowledged."

Hearing Aurora speak and act like a seasoned pro sent a surge of pride through me. She'd come so far from the scared, pregnant were-kestrel I'd first met so many months ago. Today she was doing her species—and her daughter—very proud.

Jackson must have turned his mike off, because I counted to a hundred before he spoke again. And there was no missing the tension in his voice. "Astrid?"

"I'm here," she said. "Who's in the car?"

"Well, her name badge says Hendrix, but I don't think Officer Hendrix is home."

Trepidation slithered through my gut. "What color are her eyes?" I asked.

"Bright blue," Jackson said.

Fuck, damn, and shit.

I caught Astrid's gaze and saw the same thing in her eyes that had to be reflecting in mine: shit just got real.

CHAPTER TWELVE

I started pacing the room. I needed to do something during the time it took for Jackson and his team to escort Amalie's newest avatar up to the sight of the old nature preserve, where our warriors were waiting. The two cars finally came into view on Aurora's chest-cam, and I stopped pacing in favor of cracking my knuckles.

The fact that she'd admitted who she was to Jackson made me all kinds of nervous about this, and I hated her with a blazing fury for picking Officer Hendrix. A woman who'd been so brave during the battle with the dwarves, and her open interest in the supernatural side of our city had probably made her mind an easy target for Amalie.

Amalie climbed out of the cop car, her blue eyes shining bright. Supernaturally bright, as they always did when she used a human avatar for communication.

One of the Tainted growled, and I was pretty sure that was Wyatt. He had twenty times more reasons to hate her than I did.

Jackson, Shelby, Carly and Oliver flanked Amalie as she slinked forward, moving with no haste, observing those around her. The Tainted were somewhere behind Aurora, and her gaze lingered there the longest. Not an ounce of emotion leaked through.

"I see no one here worth parlaying with," Amalie said.

Parlay? What century are we in again?

"I'm surprised you came here, sprite." Wyatt's terrible voice crackled over the speakers. "You never do your own dirty work."

She blinked once. "Such a monumental shift in the Break required a personal investigation on my part. This was, I assume, done in order to regain my attention."

"Among other things."

"And I am here. I do not, however, waste my time with beasts and children. Bring me someone worth speaking to."

Ouch.

"Aurora," Astrid said, "Tell her I'll be there in thirty minutes."

"Copy that."

I followed Astrid toward the doors without thinking. "It'll take forever to get across the city and into the mountains during rush hour," I said.

"Do you have better idea?" she snapped.

"Perhaps some of the Coni could fly back and provide transportation," Eulan said, joining our private conversation.

"In broad daylight over the city?" I asked. "Because all it takes is one fast person to put that shit on YouTube."

"You make an astute point. However, I do wish to accompany Astrid to this meeting. My people have a stake in this outcome, too."

No pun intended.

I glanced at my healing left hand, then sighed. "I can try teleporting us there. At least that will only take, like, thirty seconds."

"Have you ever teleported that distance before?" Astrid asked. "With two people attached to you?"

"No." I glanced past Eulan to Isleen, who watched silently from her seat at the table. She nodded at me. "But the Watchtower has a secret weapon we can use to my advantage."

I'd only been inside of the Sanctuary once in my afterlife. A day after my resurrection, Isleen brought me here to perform a vampire ritual that had helped me remember the last day of my first life. And I'd remembered. I'd curled into a ball and sobbed on Alex's chest as I remembered the horrific way in which I'd been tortured and died.

While First Break and the secondary hotspot that the elves were guarding were the only direct links to the other side and the source of all magic, smaller pockets of energy existed all over the city. If a human being was born over one of these hotspots, they ended up Gifted like Wyatt. Or like the body I resurrected into.

Chalice Frost had been born in the public women's bathroom back when this had been a functioning mall, because her mother Lori got stuck inside after a ceiling collapsed. Hence my handy teleporting powers.

I'd fought against the power of the Break during the Tainted summoning, and standing outside of the Sanctuary again had my tether all kinds of excited. The vampires had sealed off access when they evacuated the Watchtower, but Eulan produced a key that opened the veneered door.

He and Astrid followed me inside. The air was stale but the décor hadn't changed. Unlit, half-burned candles on the sinks and counters. Plush green carpet on the floor, three non-working toilets converted to chairs. Cozy despite the chilly air. Power rippled over my skin and vibrated through my muscles. Power so close to what I'd felt at First Break itself.

"You are certain of this?" Eulan asked.

"Yes." A part of me was terrified of what I was about to do, because I could fail. I could lose steam and teleport us into a building or drop us from the sky into the forest somewhere.

I could, but I wouldn't. I was standing on a Break, about to teleport to another Break. Magic was surging all over the place, thanks to the elves and their spell. It might be a bumpy ride, but we'd get there. Alive and in three individual pieces.

We stood in a circle in the middle of the room. I ripped bandages part of the way off my left hand so I could hold Astrid's properly.

"Hang on tight," I said. "This is going to feel weird."

I closed my eyes and pulled up every ounce of loneliness I could find: the helplessness of Wyatt dying in my arms, the grief of Tybalt bleeding out in front of me, the horror of shooting Alex in the back of the head to end his suffering. Lives lost. Friends lost. So much loss and grief and pain.

Power surged through me unlike I'd ever felt, and it ripped us apart. I held tight to my friends as we fell into the Break and moved. My healing arm screamed at me. My senses burned. Everything hurt all at once as we kept going, farther than I'd ever taken anyone before. We swam through lava that scorched every cell in my body. I had no voice to shriek.

Onward we hurtled, and I drew on memories. The empty blacktop on the other side of Jackson's car. Our destination. It was close. I pulled on everything I had, every last scrap of energy from the Break, and I took us there. Ripped us free of the Break and then hard pavement scraped my palms. Pain ripped through my skull so fiercely I nearly threw up.

Astrid and Eulan walked away, but someone was by my side. When the dizziness subsided, I blinked Carly's concerned face into focus.

"Where the hell did you come from?" she whispered.

"Headquarters. Ouch."

"Will you parlay with us?" Astrid's strong voice broke over the crowd. "Or are we, too, animals and children?"

"Your appearance is startling," Amalie replied. "I sensed magic just now. How did you arrive here?"

"Does it matter? You asked for someone worth speaking to. We're here. Parlay away."

I kind of loved Astrid for sassing the Sprite Queen.

"You risk much in bringing three Tainted into this world," Amalie said. "Their containment is will not hold indefinitely."

"You don't approve? I'm surprised. Here we thought you were totally on board with Tovin's plan to summon a Tainted that he had no hope of controlling, so that it could get loose and cause all kinds of chaos."

"That would have been amusing, yes."

"Because it would have started the downfall of mankind? Blazing the path for you and your people to reclaim the earth for themselves? Even though you don't belong here and you never did."

I wanted to see Amalie's face, to know if anything Astrid was saying had hit home. If she was surprised we knew what we did about her peoples' history.

"The elves have been quite forthcoming with information, have they not?" Amalie said. "You know more than you should."

"I know you once enslaved the vampires to do your bidding. I know that my people developed because of the magic you brought here. I know that humans are the rightful inheritor of this earth, not the Fey. I know that humans confound the Fey because they are unpredictable and ruled by their emotions, and you don't understand emotions. You don't understand why the three men behind me would risk everything to host a Tainted in order to defeat you. You don't understand why we sacrifice for those we love. It isn't in your nature anymore than giving up is in mine."

"Or mine!" I said. My voice echoed off the trees nearby.

With Carly's help I managed to stand on my own two feet. Over the hood of the car, I met Amalie's wide eyes and took a hell of a lot of satisfaction in having shocked the shit out of her.

"Surprise. Not dead," I said.

Amalie blinked. "So I see. Finally. Someone worth parlaying with."

Astrid growled.

I circled the car to stand next to Amalie and Eulan, careful not to look for Wyatt. I couldn't look at him or think about him right now, because seeing his Tainted form on a monitor and seeing it in person were two entirely different things. My head throbbed but not enough to throw my concentration.

"Could we use a more modern word than parlay?" I asked. "Debate, or negotiate, or even threaten with a fiery demise? I realize you're old as fuck and still catching up with the world, but no one has said parlay in a non-ironic way since the nineteenth century."

Which was to her as last Tuesday was to me, but whatever.

"I suspected you were alive," Amalie said. "This body's thoughts were of a girl similar to you, though your appearance has been altered somewhat. She was intrigued by you and the work that you do. It made using her for this task quite simple."

"Awesome for you. Honestly, I'm kind of surprised you came alone. I've always seen you with a bodyguard."

"You assume I am alone. You have no idea what may lay in wait."

"Let me guess. Dwarves are going to start pouring out of the woods and attacking us, right?"

"Perhaps. Or perhaps there will be no need for a battle. If you believe anything I've said to you, Evangeline, it's that sprites are peaceful. We cannot harm others directly. It is part of our nature, as much as fighting authority is in yours. But that is not a trait shared by all the Light Ones."

"Okay, cool, no one wants a fight. That's something. Why don't you do what your elf buddies wanted a long time ago, and go back to your parallel world where you belong, and leave us to this one?"

"I have no desire to do such a thing."

My fingers itched for a gun. One bullet between her eyes, and this was over. If a host body died while a sprite was still using it, the sprite died. It happened months ago with Amalie's bodyguard Jaron. I could end this so fast.

Except no, I couldn't. I'd be murdering an innocent woman. A police officer who'd been doing her job, and who was in the line of fire because a bunch of dwarves decided to lay waste to the Briar's Ridge mall.

"Look," I said, "we're not interested in another mass genocide. I don't want the sprites or any of the Fey killed down to near extinction like the Coni or the elves. We either want peaceful co-existence, or we want you the fuck off our planet."

"Peaceful co-existence between whom?" Amalie laughed, a harsh, bitter sound. "The human race is so divided you've done our work for us. You wage wars over oil, you murder in the name of false gods, you hate because of ignorance you are unwilling to fix. You waste precious resources on mindless, senseless things. You are a stain on this planet."

"We try. Every goddamn day, some of us try to make the world better. Safer."

"You can dress up the corpse however you like, but it remains dead inside."

Her skepticism and negativity were seriously damaging my calm. "Is this how parlaying works in the sprite world?" I asked. "We both state what we want, no one compromises, so nothing actually happens?"

"We are simply…what is your human slang? Putting our cards on the table."

Oh good, an analogy I can work with. "How do we know who's got the winning hand?"

"Oh my dear." Amalie's smile was wicked. "You were never even in the game."

The blue light fled her eyes, and Officer Hendrix fell to her knees.

That wasn't good.

Everyone turned outward, toward the long perimeter of trees surrounding us. Someone pressed the hilt of a blade into my right hand, and I curled my palm around it. Astrid sniffed the air. Aurora barked orders and four Coni took to the sky, skimming low over the treetops.

Nothing attacked us.

That really, really wasn't good.

Astrid touched her earpiece. "Rufus, Amalie left her avatar, but nothing's happening here."

"Where am I?" Hendrix asked.

I glanced down at her. A thin ribbon of blood ran from her nostril to her upper lips, and her dark eyes were bewildered. "You're in the middle of a really big shitstorm, that's where you are."

She finally seemed to really see me. "Oh hell, you're her. Again."

"Yeah, again."

The tremor started in my head, in that part of me that is always tethered to the Break. Then it came up through my feet as the world itself began shaking. The rushing sound of three dozen Coni rising into the air at once battled with the rumble of the quaking earth beneath me. Trees swayed. Branches cracked.

A big, dark-skinned body swept me up into hard-muscled arms. The odor of ozone made my eyes and nose sting, but I didn't struggle. I didn't have to look to know who'd grabbed me and was trying to keep me safe from the earthquake.

The shaking stopped as abruptly at it began. Air swirled above from the beat of the Coni's wings.

Wyatt placed me gently on the ground, and I dared to look at him. At the twisted angles and planes of his face, almost unrecognizable between the bi-shift and the Tainted. The pointed teeth and thick claws. The way he towered a foot above me, somehow both a monster and a protector.

"Rufus? Can you hear me?" Astrid said. "I lost contact."

I palmed my phone at the same time as Carly and Jackson. Instead of calling into Ops, though, I called Milo's phone.

"Where are you?" he asked without even a hello. "Are you trapped?"

"What? No. I'm not at HQ anymore."

"You aren't?"

"No. How are things there? We lost com with Ops."

"A giant earthquake somewhere in the city knocked out everything but backup power. Some of the walls cracked and fell over. I'm trying to get out of the dorms."

"Ten gets you twenty that was a troll attack."

"Why?"

I gave him a brief rundown of my conversation with Amalie.

"Christ, Evy, you teleported that far?" he asked. "Is your brain mush?"

"Funny. Look, just stay safe, okay? We have no idea what's happening in the city right now." And that was a scary, scary thought.

Everyone who had a phone was on it with somebody. The Tainted had clustered to the side, sticking together like the creepy-ass family they were, and I stopped trying to see my friends there because it was too big of a mind-fuck. Instead I offered Hendrix a hand to her feet.

"Do you have a working radio?" I asked.

"Yes."

"Can you find out what's going on? Strange activity in the city? Possible epicenter of that earthquake?"

"I'll try." She climbed into her car and shut the door. I watched in case she tried to turn it on. Instead she grabbed a handset from her console and started talking into it.

Astrid hung up with whomever she'd been talking and took another call. "Where are you?" Her eyes widened. "Were there people inside?"

That question got my complete attention.

"Okay, thanks Morgan." She hung up with a frustrated huff. "It looks like the focus of the troll activity and the earthquake was uptown. The Fourth Street Library is a pile of bricks and books. They hadn't opened yet so it's possible no one was killed, but there's a lot of damage for blocks in all directions."

The Fourth Street Library's roof had once been the nesting place of my gargoyle ally Max. While the gargoyles had left the city months ago, that target felt incredibly personal.

"Power is out all over uptown," Shelby reported. "And parts of Mercy's Lot."

"Things are about to get very ugly," I said. My gut was screaming it at me. "Amalie might not come at us directly, but she's got a knack for turning people against each other. Setting other species at us."

"We need to get back into the city," Astrid said. She looked up, and I realized we were missing quite a few shadows. Only Aurora, Pike, and two other Coni remained in the sky. Waiting. "Go. Keep in contact."

Aurora attempted a salute, then off they flew.

Between us, we had Jackson's car, the cop car, and the SUV that Wyatt had driven his crew up here in.

"There are reports of human looting going on in Mercy's Lot," Hendrix said, rejoining the conversation. "A lot of weird rumors are flying around on the radio, including more hairy monsters like what attacked the mall last night."

More dwarves. Great.

"Okay, load up everyone," Astrid said. "Shelby and Carly, I need you both to stay here and protect the elves. As long as they're alive, they have control of the Tainted. They—the fuck?"

I turned in a circle, the reason for her "the fuck?" becoming insanely, terrifyingly clear.

Silent as a shadow and as quick as a switch, the three Tainted were gone.

CHAPTER THIRTEEN

Thank God for contingency plans. Or in this particular case, thank Rufus.

Before they left the Watchtower, Wyatt, Marcus and Phineas were injected with our tracking dye. Even though they were probably outside of our half-mile tracking radius by the time we got the tablet booted up and the SUV headed back into the city, the chances of someone seeing a blip on the radar were—for once—kind of in our favor.

Especially if they were attracted to the violence and chaos of Mercy's Lot. My old hunting grounds.

Astrid drove while I held the tablet. Hendrix was in the backseat, probably scared out of her mind, but we couldn't leave her behind, and we couldn't turn her loose. Not when she'd seen the big, scary monsters for herself.

As we descended from the mountains and the edges of the city came into view, my first real wave of adrenaline hit. We had no idea what was happening, what was going to happen, and what sort of body count we were looking at. Human beings were easily frightened by things they didn't understand. And fear often turned to violence.

I learned that lesson the hard way while working for the Triads.

We drove into the outskirts of what would become Mercy's Lot. This part of the city I knew. I'd lived and hunted here for four years. I'd killed dozens of goblins and Halfies in these streets and alleys. I'd bled here. As a Hunter, I'd been prepared to die here. Jesse and Ash had died here.

A single red blip on the corner of my tablet map got my attention back. "Southwest."

Astrid took the next right.

The blip didn't repeat itself for several blocks, not until we passed the scorched earth ruins of what had once been a retired potato chip factory—until the gremlins who used to live there were relocated, and Kismet and her Hunters tried to blow me up in it.

Ah, memories.

"Astrid, if they're moving as a group, will I see one blip or three?" I asked.

"Depends on how closely they're moving. The tech could blur them into a single dot."

"Okay, because I only see one, which either means they're clustering, or they split up."

Split up was bad and required a lot more work on our part.

"What exactly are we tracking?" Hendrix asked.

"You really do not want an answer to that question," I replied.

"I kind of do."

I twisted around to face her. "We had three elves summon demons into the bodies of my boyfriend and two of my best friends, and they got loose."

Hendrix gave one slow blink. "Your friends or the elves?"

"Huh?"

"Which ones got loose?"

Her calm was delightfully unexpected. "My friends. They're mostly in control but it's complicated." I'd caught her listening to my phone explanation to Milo, so she had some of the back story. "I'm sorry you got mixed up in this mess."

"Sounds like you can use all the help you can get. I have a sidearm, a baton, and a taser."

I glanced at Astrid, who shrugged. At this point, Hendrix had seen and heard enough to be our newest Watchtower recruit. It would be nice to have a cop ally again. "Look, officer, the three men out there who look uber-scary? We don't want to kill them, we only want to find out what they're doing. The Tainted possessing them agreed to help us, and running off on their own wasn't part of the plan."

Hendrix's lips quirked. "The best laid plans, huh?"

"No kidding." Okay, it was official: I liked her.

Traffic thickened a bit as we left the bones of the old industrial yards behind for the tightly-packed apartments and strip malls that made up the heart of Mercy's Lot. The blip continued its southward pace. At the intersection of Cottage Place and Peach Street, they ceased forward motion.

"I think they stopped." I told Astrid how to get there, and the location made my gut cramp. "Something got their attention."

The SUV slammed to a stop at the next left because of standstill traffic. It was a one-way street, and someone came up behind, blocking us in.

I grabbed the door handle.

"Let me come with you," Hendrix said. "A uniform might help."

"In this neighborhood? Stay in the car."

Astrid shifted into park but left the engine running. "Please, stay with the car, officer."

We both abandoned ship to investigate the cause for the traffic snarl. Half a block from our destination I heard the first roar of an angry beast. The screaming got louder, more insistent. I turned the corner at a dead run and nearly slammed into a crowd of gawkers.

The front windows of Sally's Diner were smashed in, the door wide open. I went in without thinking, blade in hand. The sharp tang of blood mixed with the odors of fryer grease and coffee. At least a dozen bodies littered the floor and booths. I stared at the back booth where I'd watched a private investigator friend named James Reilly devour many a plate of pancakes.

His dead body wasn't there, but an elderly man was.

Four of the bodies on the floor were Halfies. Those had been ripped to shreds.

I found a waitress cowering under the front counter and urged her to come out. "What happened?"

"At first it was these four punk kids," the woman replied. She took in the carnage and turned a little green. "They were, ah, being mouthy. Loud. Then this one kid, he grabs Teddy, the cook, yeah? Grabs him by the neck and just…bites his throat. The other three go at my customers, and it was awful, and then these three big…things. I heard them mostly, because I hid. I was so fucking scared."

"It's okay, hiding was smart."

"They killed the Halfies and kept going," Astrid said. "That's a good sign."

"Doesn't help us find them, though."

"What's a Halfie?" the waitress asked. "Is that a gang name?"

I rolled my eyes. "Something like that. Come on."

Traffic must have gotten going again, because Hendrix had the SUV idling outside the diner when we emerged. "Your people are moving again," she shouted out the open passenger side window.

I deferred shotgun to Astrid and climbed into the backseat. Every SUV had weapons stored under the seat and I produced a handgun and a switchblade on Astrid's orders. She liked to fight in her true form, but I couldn't very well run around the city with a giant jungle cat as backup.

That would be weird.

We drove down Cottage Place, directly west now. Past my old Triad apartment. The road eventually dead-ended on a north-south highway that ran along the Black River, but our quarry stopped moving again six blocks from that road.

We saw the commotion while we were still a block away. Hendrix pulled onto the sidewalk in between two out of service parking meters so Astrid and I could get out. Up the road, the sound of gunshots sent a chill down my spine. No cop cars, so someone must have pulled a personal piece.

Another business had shattered front windows, this time a Mexican grocery store. Crashes and screams. Another gunshot.

Astrid grabbed my arm before I could barrel inside and shoved me against the brick building. Onlookers had phones up, probably recording, but whatever. She peeked in through the broken glass.

"Store's a wreck," she said. "One man behind the cash register with a gun. Looks like more's going down in the rear. Hard to see."

Astrid slid inside first, gun in hand. I followed behind. The terrified teenage boy behind the counter turned his aim on us. "*Policía*," Astrid said.

He seemed to buy it, because he ducked down to hide.

A bloody body came sailing at us and hit the cash register with a sickening splat. The teenager screamed, and then bolted out the front door. Streaked hair and nubby incisors. Fresh Halfie. I had no idea where our guys were heading, but at least they were taking care of business on the way.

Frustration mounting, I said to hell with it all, and shouted, "Wyatt Truman! Stop fucking running from me!"

I felt Astrid's eye roll.

Someone roared in the rear of the store. Probably Wyatt's inner wolf, responding instinctively to his mate's order. The Tainted had a plan of its own, and I couldn't imagine the mental battle going on in Wyatt's head.

Metal squealed.

I took off running, dodging fallen displays and seas of broken glass. All kinds of things crunched under my feet. Something thudded in the distance. More dead Halfies, a few random shoppers. Blood streaked a swinging door that said something in Spanish. I shoved through, past racks of boxed product, to find the sun streaming in through what used to be a big back door.

No sign of our guys.

"Damn it, Truman!" My voice bounced down the empty access alley that reeked of garbage and piss.

Bloody footprints, spaced wide, led east down the alley. I followed them, determined to find my boyfriend and his Tainted cohorts. Halfies were suddenly on the warpath, and I had no doubt in my mind that Amalie had somehow orchestrated these organized attacks on places where innocents were likely to cluster.

Easy targets.

The footprints faded until they were gone. I'd followed them a good four blocks east, and now I'd lost not only them, but also Astrid. She hadn't followed me into the alley. Frustrated and thirsty, I retraced my steps back to the grocery store.

Astrid and the SUV were gone.

"You are shitting me," I said to the sky.

It made sense. The guys were moving; I was gone. They had to follow. Not like I couldn't handle myself in

Mercy's Lot. I did my best to disappear into the flow of foot traffic, people going to work or going home after a long night on the street corner. My half-bandaged arm didn't do me any favors, so I tugged the rest of it off. My hand was still pretty gross looking, the skin craggy and red, almost like a bad burn. The tendons and muscles mostly worked okay, even though it ached like a bitch in that moment.

Three blocks from the grocery store, my phone rang.

"We haven't lost them," Astrid said. "They're still moving south, pretty consistently."

"And taking out Halfies along the way. This is insane."

"I know."

They clearly had a direction in mind. Something from the elves' conversation with the Tainted down in that cave poked at my brain. "Astrid, did you know that Brevin was going to offer to give back the Tainted we contained as payment for helping us stop Amalie?"

"We discussed it. He felt it would be their best incentive to cooperate."

"Where is it being stored?"

Her end went silent.

"It's at the Watchtower, isn't it?" I said.

"Yes."

A Watchtower recently damaged by the earthquake and full of wounded who had no idea what was coming. "Call Rufus right now and warn him. Then get in touch with Aurora and tell her to meet me, um." I looked at my location. Apartments. Fire escapes. "Meet me on the roof of Glennview Apartments on Riverside Road."

"I will. I'll let you know if we intercept them."

"Thanks."

The fire escape took longer to ascend than I'd have liked, thanks to my hand, and I wasn't risking the energy suck of a teleport. The building was only five stories, but I was exhausted and in desperate need of twenty hours of uninterrupted sleep. Once I collapsed on the tarpaper roof to catch my breath, I called Milo again.

"You guys get power back yet?" I asked when he picked up after way too many rings.

"No, but we have some generators going." He said something to someone else. "Sorry, it's pretty chaotic right now. Everyone's been accounted for, though."

"Good. Listen, Astrid is filling Rufus in on this but I need you to find the pups and sit on them."

"Not literally, right?"

"If you have to, yes." I told him my suspicions about the direction of our Tainted friends. "If the pups realize that Wyatt is distressed or angry, it will affect their mood. It may force them to shift or do something dangerous."

"Like bite me? Are you crazy?"

"They've sworn to me and Wyatt they won't bite anyone. Please? Wyatt's mood will affect theirs, and if they get upset, it might make everything worse for Wyatt. Things are awful enough right now."

"Okay, I'll find them. I think they're still in the infirmary helping. Are you coming back?"

"As soon as possible. Astrid is still tailing them with the tracking dye, and Rufus will know once they hit the perimeter."

"Goodie."

"Be safe."

"You too, Evy."

My thirst became more desperate in the few minutes I paced the apartment building roof, waiting for my ride. And my vantage point sucked. I was surrounded by taller buildings on three sides, so I had no idea what was going on in the streets below. Police sirens drifted around me, along with the occasional scream.

The city was at war with itself, and I couldn't do anything to stop the carnage because I had three demon hosts to intercept.

Aurora swooped down out of nowhere, her blade streaked with different colors of blood. Some splattered her chest and neck, making her look the part of the battle-weary warrior that she now was. "I was told you needed a fast ride across town."

"I'd appreciate it, yeah."

"Assume the position."

While she sheathed her blade, I crossed my arms and tucked my hands beneath my armpits. Aurora stepped up behind me and looped her thin arms around my waist, holding my back tightly against her chest. On a rush of air and great flap of her wings, we were airborne. Soaring low over buildings, she flew us with a speed I didn't expect. The wind rushed around us, chilling my face and arms, and it was almost difficult to breathe.

Out of Mercy's Lot, we crossed the Black River where it met with the Anjean River, and she followed it south. Once upon a time the rivers were used as shipping routes, and some of those old docks still stood, aging and falling into the water. To my right were the glittering skyscrapers and business offices of uptown. To my left the dreary, poverty-stricken homes of the east side.

I'd never seen so much of the city from this vantage point—the stark differences of two areas separated by nothing more than a waterway.

The white U-shape of the Watchtower came into view. Magic rippled across my skin as we crossed the border spell. Aurora landed in front of the main entrance, instead of the roof, which turned out to be a good idea. A welcoming committee in the form of a grizzly bear, Paul with a rifle that I hoped was loaded with sedative darts, and two more Coni warriors.

It took me a few seconds of orienting to gravity again to realize the bear was Dr. Vansis.

No one looked scared, only pissed off and ready for a fight.

"Tainted plan not working out so well?" Paul asked. His shoulder had been re-bandaged and was blood-free.

"We had an unexpected hiccup," I replied. "Rufus fill everyone in?"

Lots of nods.

"Should we remove the crystallized Tainted from the Watchtower?" Aurora asked.

One of the Coni, a woman with snow-white wings and matching white hair, stepped forward. She held a metal box the size of a basketball, and even from six feet away, I felt the power inside of it. "We are prepared to do that very thing should violence erupt," she said.

"Which forward thinker in the group came up with that plan?" I asked.

"I did," Milo said, emerging from the shadows. "Rufus agreed."

"What are you doing here?" Besides the fact that he was leaning heavily on a cane and his color was awful, he had another job to do.

"I talked to the boys, and they agreed to let me lock them inside the interrogation room, just in case. They're already stressed, and they understand the need for desperate measures."

"Oh." That had been unexpectedly reasonable of them. "Okay then. But still, what are you doing here? Things could get dangerous."

He glared. I didn't care. Not even when Paul handed him a second rifle.

"How in control of our people are the Tainted?" Paul asked.

"We're not sure," I said. "They took off without a word, and even though they've stopped a few times to slaughter Halfies, they are definitely on a mission south. Most likely here. The Tainted are more rational than Amalie led us to believe. They know that we have a family member locked in that box, and they want him back. Hopefully our people are in charge enough to keep this from getting violent."

I couldn't stand to watch Wyatt torn apart by bullets or blades if he turned against us and started hurting innocents.

It would kill me, too.

I swapped my blade to my left hand so I could answer a call from Astrid.

"They're less than a mile from the Watchtower," she said. "We're making good time finally but they'll beat us to you."

"Thanks, Astrid."

I repeated that to the group, pocketed my phone, then switched knife hands. "Just so no one's surprised," I said, "they're really, really ugly. And purple."

"Purple?" Paul said.

"Quite purple," the white-haired Coni said. "And among us."

I pivoted, unsurprised to see the three Tainted slowing from a run to a long-strided walk as they made their way across the inner parking lot to us. My stomach still twisted unhappily at the sight of my lover so deformed and my friends as potential new enemies. The Coni woman took to the sky in a whoosh of air that swirled around us. Her shadow lingered above, so she wasn't fleeing. Only putting herself and the box out of range.

The Tainted didn't rush us or attack. They stalked toward our group, a fuming trio of hate, anger and determination, spackled with drying blood from various kills. We formed a line, myself in the center, Milo off to the side so he could brace himself with the doorway.

The trio stopped a few feet away, Wyatt on point with Marcus and Phineas flanking him. Marcus's head swiveled, and I knew the moment he spotted Milo by the way his nostrils flared.

"Why did you leave the Olsmill site?" I asked, reaching for some of my own anger to keep any tremors out of my voice. "You agreed to assist us in defeating the Fey."

"And we will abide by that bargain," Wyatt said in his inhumanly deep voice.

"By sprinting through the city and coming here?"

"We relieved you of several of the half-Bloods who plague this city. You're welcome."

That tiny sparkle of Wyatt came through in those words. "Why did you come here? There are too many innocent lives inside. We won't allow you to enter."

"Entry is not necessary to acquire what we want."

Fuck me.

Wyatt. Sanctuary. Gifted. The box.

"Get that out of here now!" I shouted to the Coni in the sky, even as the first ripples of Break power caressed my skin. Not from my tap, though.

From Wyatt's.

He raised his clawed right hand, palm up. Too fucking calm.

A red feather appeared in his right shoulder, and he ignored it. The second made him drop his hand and sway, no box in sight. Marcus and Phineas snarled, but made no move to attack. Probably because Wyatt hadn't toppled over or even fallen to his knees, and one of those darts was supposed to be able to take down a charging buffalo.

"Really?" I snapped. "What was the plan? Summon the box, free your son, and then go tear apart my city?"

Wyatt's eyes blazed. "No. We simply do not trust your kind to withhold your end of the bargain. We were ensuring our kin was returned before we did your bidding."

"My kind? Truman, I was listening in when the elves made their deal with the Tainted, and I am telling you demons inside my friends that we will abide by the bargain. Help us defeat the Fey? You get your family back. Period."

Several long, painful seconds passed.

"I believe her," Phineas said. "She will return Darash to us."

"She had better," Marcus snarled.

Yeah, because poor Marcus was housing Darash's wife. Good thing no one besides me and Milo knew that little factoid.

I glanced across the parking lot toward the street. "Shouldn't Astrid have been back by now?"

As if in reply to my question, a distant screech of tires was instantly followed by a dull crunch and rumble. I ran toward it without thinking, unsurprised when all three Tainted went right past me. At the end of the mall structure, they paused for a moment, then angled to the right. When I caught up, I made a sharp turn and nearly stumbled.

The SUV had smashed right into the side of the old department store, hard enough to accordion the front end. I could see the remains of at least two goblins poking out between the stone and the vehicle's grill. Another one lay on the ground, and one swift smash from Phineas's foot splatted its head into bits. Wyatt made fast work of two more goblins who were trying to run off.

Marcus tore off the passenger side door. I got as close to him as I dared while he gently lifted Astrid out of the front seat. Blood poured down her face from a cut I couldn't see, and she was struggling to stay conscious.

"Came out of nowhere," she said. "Little shits. Out of nowhere."

I circled the SUV to the driver's side. The window was busted, and Hendrix was draped over the steering wheel, but her fucking door wouldn't open. I yanked helplessly at the handle, one second away from screaming my frustration, when Wyatt pulled it right off. Heart hammering, I pressed my fingers to her neck.

Steady pulse.

The seatbelt wouldn't budge. Wyatt ripped that like it was paper, then gently removed her from the front seat. Her head lolled back, exposing several long, bleeding scratches on her neck. I couldn't see her crashing the car on purpose, but fear and pain did things to a person's sense of direction. A goblins probably smashed through the window, gored her neck, and panic mode took over.

"Infirmary," Marcus growled.

"You aren't allowed inside the Watchtower," I said. "Aurora?"

She took Astrid from Marcus and flew off. The other Coni took Hendrix from Wyatt and did the same. I wanted to follow to make sure Astrid was okay, but the current situation needed my attention.

And I had no idea what to do next. So I called Rufus.

"Ops," he said.

"It's Stone. I'm outside with the three Tainted. They're finally behaving, so what should I do with them?"

"If they're on a leash, we need them in Mercy's Lot. I can't keep up with police reports of unusual attacks. A giant cloud of insects near Grove Park. Businesses being ransacked downtown by furry creatures with claws."

"Fantastic. Listen, we're—"

Bear-Vansis roared.

I turned around.

The Three Tainted were almost out of sight already, moving north at breakneck speed. Heading toward Mercy's Lot.

"You have got to be shitting me," I said.

"What?" Rufus asked.

"Therian hearing, I guess. The Tainted are off and running toward danger."

"Alone?"

"Dude, they have like, cheetah land speed."

Rufus made a noise. "Fine, let them go fight it out. I'll make sure our teams on the ground keep an eye out for them."

"Don't you mean 'get a car and follow them, Stone'?"

"No. We're a mess, too, and I need you here."

I glared into the distance. "Fine."

Instinct told me to disobey that order and go into the city anyway. Another deeper gut feeling told me to stay. Nowhere was safe today, and I had too many injured allies in a damaged building to risk leaving them.

After today, nothing will ever be the same.

CHAPTER FOURTEEN

I had no idea where all of the camping lanterns came from, but they were spaced far enough apart up and down the corridors that I could walk freely. And see the damage. Cracks in the walls and floor tiles. Broken glass in some of the old storefront windows. The structure itself had to be sound, or Rufus would have evacuated by now.

As much as I wanted to check in with the pups first, I headed straight for Ops with Milo. Bear Vansis trundled past us, heading back to the infirmary and his new patients. Everyone else had stayed behind at the entrance to guard it, because God knew what else might attack today.

The silence didn't compute right away. I was used to the Watchtower being full of activity at all hours. Today the corridors were nearly empty. The bulk of our active force was out in the city, doing their best to save lives. Everyone still here to was too wounded to fight, so they were either in the infirmary, or in their rooms resting. The quiet reminded me too much of my first time here with Isleen and Alex all those months ago.

Ops was a special mess. Several workstations had fallen over, and one of the big wall monitors lay on the floor in pieces. The hum of a generator joined the chatter of the half-dozen people inside, and they were all working around a single functioning computer.

"Any news on Astrid or Hendrix?" I asked.

"Nothing yet," Rufus replied without looking up from his screen. He had a map of the city up, with a lot of red and blue dots all over the place, but mostly clustered in Mercy's Lot. "Say again, Gina?"

Kismet was reporting from the field. I tried really hard to stave off a pang of jealousy.

"Okay, thanks." Rufus glanced up. "A group of Halfies that attacked a grocery store have been dealt with."

Meaning killed. "Whoever planned these attacks was smart," I said. "They're going after locations where humans gather in large groups. Makes them easier targets."

"Agreed. Every school in the city is on lockdown, including the university. The police are overwhelmed, and now I'm hearing reports of civilians taking to the streets with guns."

Exactly the kind of disaster the Triads had been formed to prevent. At least, that's what we'd always believed. Amalie had wanted this sort of war all along, only she'd gone into things hoping that humans would end up standing alone, with vampires and Therians as our enemies. We fucked with her plan by standing together as allies.

I just hoped we could get this shitstorm under control before too many lives were lost.

"What do you need me to do?" I asked.

"We sustained one coordinated attack already today," Rufus replied. "I need you here in case we're targeted again. Get something to eat, weapon up, and then come back."

The idea of a nice stack of pancakes was overwhelmingly pleasant, but my nerves were strung so tight I was afraid of barfing it all back up. I could be useful and feed the pups, though. It gave me an excuse to check in on them.

"Yeah okay." I nudged Milo with my elbow. "Come on, gimpy. Keep me company."

As much as I wanted a hot shower, with my luck that would be the moment the shit hit the fan. So we went to the empty cafeteria and settled at a table near the entrance. I forced down a bowl of raisin bran, while Milo picked at a bagel.

"Seeing the change on a computer and seeing it in person isn't the same," Milo said. His voice was soft but real grief lingered in those words.

"I know. But our guys are still in there. I see it in how Wyatt reacts to me, and how Marcus reacted when Astrid was hurt."

"For how much longer, though? Hours? Days?"

"I don't know. However long it takes."

"You have so much more faith than I do. Sometimes I really hate you for that."

I shrugged. "I should have died half a dozen times these past couple of months. Somehow, for some reason, I keep on ticking. I can't guess at the future. All I can do is have faith that we'll be okay, because otherwise I'd curl up into a ball and scream until my throat bleeds."

"That's reasonable, I guess." He smashed a bagel crumb into the table with his thumb. "It's how I feel, too, most days. Especially recently."

"We're still only human, pal. Even we have limits to the violence and heartache that we can stand before we break completely."

"Evangeline?" Peter's voice echoed in the quiet room.

My chair scraped as I stood, surprised as hell to see all three of the pups standing in the cafeteria entrance. "What are you doing out?"

They glanced at each other in joint confusion.

"A woman let us out," Peter replied. "She said that you told her we no longer needed to hide."

An awful, insidious idea slithered into the back of my mind. "What woman?"

"I'm not sure. She was wearing a police uniform, though."

"Fucking hell. What color were her eyes?"

"Um." Peter swallowed hard, cowering a bit like a kid who knew he'd messed up and expected punishment. "Blue, I think. She squinted a lot and it was dark."

I grabbed my phone and dialed.

"Ops," Rufus said.

"We have a big problem. Amalie tagged along for the ride when Officer Hendrix drove through our barrier spell. She's inside the Watchtower."

"How do you know?"

"Because she released the Lupa pups." My irrational brain started playing the chorus from "Who Let the Dogs Out?" and I nearly laughed. "We need to find Hendrix."

"No need to look far," said the object of my ire.

The pups all jumped and scrambled closer to my table. I was around the other side in a flash, inserting myself between her and the others. Hendrix eased into the cafeteria, her right hand raised, gun aimed at my head. Blue fire in her eyes.

Rufus's voice squawked over my abandoned phone.

"You're a tricky bitch, aren't you?" I asked.

"I saw a very intriguing opportunity to observe this Watchtower of yours from the inside," Amalie replied. "I could not resist it."

"So you came and you saw. Go away."

"So soon?"

I resisted the very real urge to growl at her. "You might as well put the gun down. We both know you won't use it."

"You're so certain of that?"

"You've said over and over how sprites can't cause physical harm to other living creatures. That a lie too?"

"Perhaps so." She shifted several feet to the side, then waved the muzzle of the gun at Milo. "Human. Close and lock these doors."

Milo glanced at me. Amalie had a gun with enough bullets to kill all five of us. No sense in taking chances. I nodded at him.

We'd installed garage-style doors in case of invasion or emergency, so this section could be cut off and protected. Milo pulled the metal gate down first and it clicked into place. Voices bounced down the corridor toward us, cut off by the second door snapping in. Closing us off from our friends.

"Now what?" I asked. "Pancake breakfast?"

"You will joke until your final death, won't you, Evangeline?" Amalie asked.

"Probably. Snark keeps me from losing my mind. What do you want?"

"A test."

"Will this test be multiple choice?"

Milo grunted.

"You are growing tiresome," Amalie said. "You are also not involved in this test. You, child." She pointed the gun at John, and every muscle in my body went taut. "Come here."

Peter growled, and I held up a hand to shush him. Amalie was up to something, but she still hadn't physically hurt anyone. This was some kind of mind game, I was sure of it. I just didn't want to risk our lives if it turned out she could actually pull that trigger.

Someone banged on the other side of the door.

John took three steps closer to Amalie, shoulders squared, chin up.

"Closer," Amalie said.

He stopped an arm's reach away, which put him about four long steps from me.

"Do you fear me?" she asked.

"I fear your actions," he replied, voice strong. Not a single tremor, and pride warmed my chest for his bravery. "You're threatening people I love. People I will fight for."

"Fascinating. You would fight for that human?" She tilted her chin at me.

"Yes, I would."

"Even though she participated in the hunt for and murder of your brothers?"

Mark made a soft noise.

John didn't flinch. "We attacked her loved ones first. She was protecting those she loved from a very real threat. She stood up for us and helped prevent our execution by the Assembly of Clan Elders. I will fight for her."

"A rational decision." Amalie smiled, and that was fucking creepy. "I was uncertain how feral Lupa pups would adapt the human world. I admit, I had hoped for more chaos from you seven, but you were briefly useful."

Milo's phone rang.

"So you came all this way to chit chat with the boys?" I asked. "You could have saved yourself a trip and called."

Amalie ignored me in favor of turning the gun so she grasped the barrel. She held the butt out to John. "Take it."

John didn't hesitate in grasping the butt of the gun. Amalie's fingers brushed John's and in that horrifying moment, I realized what she was doing.

"John, let go!"

Hendrix's eyes closed and she slumped to the ground with a dull thud. John pivoted neatly, gun barrel pressed to the underside of his chin. His naturally blue eyes now glowed with an unnatural light.

Fuck, fuck, fuck and damn.

"Brother?" Peter asked. "What are you doing?"

"The sprite is in control of him," I said. A brand-new rage heated my chest and set my heart galloping.

"Yes, she is," Amalie said, the confirmation an awful thing to hear in John's voice. "And she will kill this host unless you do as I tell you."

"She won't kill him." I planted myself in between John's body and his brothers. "She'll kill herself. It's an empty threat."

Blue eyes flashed. "Will you take that risk with your brother's life? Haven't you lost enough of your kin to these humans?"

"What do you want us to do?" Peter asked.

Amalie pointed at Hendrix's prone form. "Bite her."

Ice water trickled down my spine. The boys had promised to never, ever bite another human being. Their bite would infect Hendrix with the Lupa virus, and it would very likely kill her. Wyatt had barely survived it himself.

"We swore we wouldn't bite again," Mark said. "We promised our Alpha."

"Is that promise worth your brother's life?" Amalie asked. Her finger shifted from the trigger guard to the trigger itself. "She's human. Her fear will see your kind destroyed. This city is in chaos. Once the human authorities know of your existence, they'll have you executed. Or worse, exploited for experimentation."

The boys' collective fear filled the room, a palpable thing that rippled over my skin and made my tether to the Break sing.

"You'll be chained, cut up, mutilated and then, when their scientists have no more use for you, you'll be killed."

A long, low growl made goosebumps rise on my neck and shoulders. I glanced over my shoulder.

Oh fuck.

Both Mark and Peter had bi-shifted. Despite their bravado, they were still teenage boys living in a world that hated them, surrounded by other species that feared them, and their kin was being threatened. Their entire existence was being threatened. I needed Wyatt so badly in that moment, and he was lost to me. Fighting another battle set in motion by the queen sprite bitch in front of me.

"She won't shoot John," I said in my best Alpha voice. "She *can't* kill him."

Amalie pressed the gun harder into John's throat. "Bite her."

"Don't."

"Now!"

Peter lunged first.

I tackled him hard, my shoulder digging into his midsection, and we rolled into the serving counter. Plates and dishes rattled. I only caught of flash of Mark dashing past, and then the sound of thudding flesh before Peter's thrashing sent my head into the cabinet. He snapped at my face without actually biting.

"Stop it now!" I said. "She can't hurt him! If she could have, she'd have bitten Hendrix herself."

"Goddamn it," Milo shouted. "Shit, listen to her."

Amalie started laughing, a haunting sound that turned almost freakish with John's still-changing voice. She sounded so damned pleased with herself that my gut cramped.

Peter tossed me off him, but didn't attack. He remained in a crouch, his gaze fixed on the other side of the doorway. I rolled to my knees, immediately searching for Hendrix. She still lay on the floor, unconscious, untouched. Past her, Mark had lost his bi-shift, but he had blood on his mouth.

My entire world tilted sideways.

Milo sat on the ground, his right hand clutching his left shoulder, his expression so completely blank I nearly missed the threads of blood on his cheek and fingers.

"No," I said.

His gaze met mine, and the genuine fear that blossomed in his face brought tears to my eyes.

"Goodbye, Evangeline," Amalie said.

A rush of magic snapped through the room, and then John fell to his knees. The gun clattered to the floor.

"I'm so sorry," Mark said. "So sorry."

I couldn't move. If I moved, it would be real and I didn't want it to be real. "Milo?"

Milo nodded as the first pink roses of fever bloomed on his cheeks.

He was infected.

CHAPTER FIFTEEN

My ass was numb from being parked on a plastic chair for who knew how long when Astrid knocked on the door frame. I hadn't seen her since Marcus raced her from the crashed SUV to the infirmary. She looked good as new, except for a big bruise on her forehead and her obvious distress.

Join the club.

"How is he?" she asked.

I glanced at the bed. Dr. Vansis had put Milo into a medically induced coma once the fever began to swing into the danger zone. In the weeks since Wyatt's infection, Dr. Vansis hadn't managed to create an antidote for the Lupa virus, but he'd studied it enough to apply certain human anti-virals to fight it. To hopefully keep it from killing Milo.

Wyatt had been lucky to survive his infection and find a way to live with it.

I had no idea if Milo would wake up, or who he'd been if he did.

"He's alive," I replied.

"I'm so sorry. I had no idea Amalie had gotten back inside of Officer Hendrix."

"Not your fault."

It wasn't, and I didn't blame Astrid. I didn't blame Mark, either, even though Milo's blood was very literally on his lips. Mark had been goaded into an action he would *not* have taken if John's life wasn't at risk. Mark had been so terrified of my reaction after the initial bite that he'd flatted out on the floor and exposed his throat.

But in those first few minutes, I hadn't been able to think about the boys. All I could think about was Milo. Getting the doors up so help could get in. Insisting Milo be carried to the infirmary so his heart rate didn't go up and pump the virus through his system faster. Milo had gone feverish and flu-ish faster than Wyatt had, which scared me. Wyatt had been bitten worse and the wound coated in Lupa blood.

Was the virus somehow more powerful in bi-shift? Or was it because Milo was still physically recovering from all kinds of wounds, and he wasn't in top shape?

"We haven't told anyone in the field," Astrid said.

"Gina doesn't know?"

"I need her focused on getting the city back under control. There's nothing she can do for Milo right now, except fight against the chaos Amalie is trying to cause."

I hated how right she was about that. Kismet would want to return to the Watchtower, and she couldn't do anything except what I was doing—sitting around worrying over whether my best friend was going to live or die.

"He's only twenty," I said. "He's survived more pain and heartbreak than so many people who live to be a hundred. Milo isn't allowed to go out like this."

"He's survived because he's a fighter. A warrior. Believe in that strength, Evangeline."

"I do." Something else in her expression, something guarded, made me ask, "What else is going on?"

She winced. "We think the Lupa pups' fear is leaking over to Wyatt somehow. We're hearing that his actions are becoming more erratic, less controlled."

"He can sense their emotions, and all of the power inside of him from the Tainted is probably strengthening that bond. The boys are terrified that they'll be executed for this."

"That isn't my call to make."

"I know. It's the Assembly's call." And Marcus's cousin was the Felia Clan Elder.

This is going to be bad.

"The boys are safe," Astrid said. "They went back into lockup willingly, and they're being guarded by one of the Coni."

"Safe for now."

"I know you care about them, but they swore to the Assembly they wouldn't bite another human. Mark broke that promise. Peter intended to."

"Tell me something I don't know!" I reeled my temper back in. Astrid wasn't a fair target. "I hate everything about this. Amalie tricked them. It isn't Mark's fault."

"Unfortunately, that isn't your call to make."

I stood up, ass smarting from being sat on for too damned long. Milo's cheeks blazed with fever, while the rest of his body was pale. Clammy. His chest rose and fell with the steady hiss of a ventilator—a precaution, Dr. Vansis had said. Another loved one of mine fighting for his life, and I was done.

Done.

"I won't do this anymore," I said, more to him than to Astrid. "I won't sit around and wait for Amalie's next move. I can't."

"What are you going to do?"

"She attacked us in our home. She struck at our heart." I turned to face Astrid, determination settling deep in my gut. "It's time we took the fight to her."

Astrid tilted her head. "How?"

"Amalie has lied to us about a lot of things. What if she lied when she said the Fey were leaving the city? What if they're still in First Break, holed up in their little rock rooms, laughing at the way we're running all over the city cleaning up their messes? What if everything going on right now is one giant distraction?"

"It's possible. But we checked the tunnel you said that you and Wyatt used to return from First Break. It's gone."

"That's not the only way down."

"Trolls?"

I shook my head. "Me."

"You?"

"Yes. I'll teleport the Tainted right to Amalie's front door."

I'd used the power of the Sanctuary to teleport myself and Astrid miles away to the mountains north of the city. Months ago during a thunderstorm, Wyatt and I had combined our taps to the Break in order to summon half a Jeep full of weapons into a cabin. Together in the Sanctuary, with the power of the Tainted and our taps to the Break, I knew deep in my bones I could get the four of us to First Break.

First I needed to get Wyatt and Marcus not to kill each other over what went down with Mark and Milo.

I stayed with Milo until I got word from Astrid that our three hosts were being brought back to the Watchtower. We weren't going to lay the plan on them until they were here. The fewer people who knew, the smaller the chance of the Fey somehow getting wind. As it was, Astrid had only told Rufus, and he was on board.

So instead of pacing Milo's room, I paced up and down the corridor in front of Ops, alive with nervous energy and adrenaline. Aurora stood nearby with a tranq rifle carefully hidden behind her wings, just in case things got ugly.

I was pretty sure things were going to get ugly.

Mid-pace, the short hairs on the back of my neck prickled with awareness, and I stopped moving. I knew they were coming before the trio of Tainted turned the corner, trailed closely by Kismet and Pike. The three

Tainted zeroed in on me right away, and I realized my first mistake in the way Wyatt's eyes narrowed.

I had some of Milo's blood on my shirt.

"I'm not hurt," I said, hoping to put Wyatt's immediate worry to rest.

Marcus's nostrils flared. "It's Milo's. What happened?"

"He's alive, but he is hurt."

I didn't protest when Marcus broke from the group and sprinted down the corridor for the infirmary. He was going to scare the hell out of Dr. Vansis. Kismet followed him.

"What happened?" Wyatt asked.

He and Phineas stopped in front of me, and it took everything in me not to cower. They somehow seemed even uglier than before, their purplish skin glistening with flecks of drying blood.

"Amalie got through our barrier spell," I said. "She tricked the pups into thinking John's life was in danger. She goaded them into reacting out of fear and instinct, instead of rationally."

Wyatt's anger turned to alarm. "One of them bit Milo."

"Yes."

"That's an unfortunate turn of events," Phineas said.

"You think? Dr. Vansis induced a coma, and he's trying some anti-virals."

"But even if he survives," Wyatt said, "he'll be changed. And the boys will be to blame."

"Bingo."

He gazed down the hall toward the infirmary, seemingly unaware of the occasional terrified look being thrown his way by others going about their business. "Who was it?"

"Does it matter? They'll all be condemned as one, Wyatt. They're terrified right now."

"I know. I sense their fear."

"You retrieved us from the field to inform us of this?" Phineas asked. "A phone call would have taken less time."

Hello, Mister Snippy.

"No," I replied. "I brought you three back so I can use the power of the Sanctuary, as well as Wyatt's tap to the Break, to teleport us all to First Break."

"Oh. Why?"

"Because I think that Amalie is still there. It's her home. It's the doorway to the world she left behind. And I'm fucking sick of standing around waiting for her to attack. It's time for us to go on the offensive."

Wyatt and Phineas exchanged a look, their expressions difficult to read. Wyatt wouldn't want me to take such a huge risk. Phineas would see that it was the only way. The Tainted in each of them was probably ecstatic over the idea of a little in-person payback.

"I'm not saying we go down there so you guys can rip the wings off every pixie you see," I added. "But if we can get to Amalie, maybe pluck a few jewels loose to show her how serious we are, it could stop this."

"The only way to stop this is to kill Amalie," Phineas said. "To kill the beast you lop off its head, you do not poke it with a stick and hope it goes away. Amalie holds much sway over the Fey Council. Eliminating her shifts the focus of the Fey from us to other things."

"Agreed." I looked at Wyatt. "What do you think? Ready to go back to First Break?"

Wyatt nodded. "I am. One last battle by your side."

Considering the last time we were at First Break, Wyatt got the shock of his life when he realized that Tovin planned to stick a Tainted into Wyatt once I died a second time, the irony kind of painted itself all over the place.

"Great," I said. "Now we just need to get—"

"Marcus! Wait!" Kismet's voice.

The heavy footsteps clued me in to Marcus's barrel down the corridor before I could turn around, and then I didn't need to because he slammed into Wyatt like a wrecking ball. The two massive men tumbled to the ground, Marcus's hands around Wyatt's throat. His inner Felia drove his anger and need for vengeance against the Alpha of the Lupa who'd hurt the man he'd claimed as his own.

Aurora shot Marcus in the back with a tranq. Marcus didn't notice it at first, his entire focus on choking Wyatt. Phineas wrapped his arms around Marcus's shoulders and yanked. The drug was enough to loosen Marcus's grip, and Phineas managed to peel him off my Tainted boyfriend.

"I'll kill them with my bare hands," Marcus roared, still stuck in Phin's firm hold.

"It wasn't their fault," I said. "It's Amalie's. She did this to Milo."

Marcus snarled at me, and that got Wyatt on his feet and in my personal space.

"This needs to wait," Phineas said. "Anger and vengeance is for this is a task for later. Once Amalie is dealt with and your husband is returned to us."

I blinked my way through that one, until I realized the Tainted was talking about the one we had on ice. Dueling personalities was confusing as hell.

"Phin is right," Astrid said. She and Rufus had emerged from Ops together to survey the scene. "Marcus, listen to Evangeline's plan."

He did, and by the time I finished, Phineas had released him. Marcus was still shooting death glares at Wyatt, but he seemed on board. Wyatt, meanwhile, had shifted his focus from Marcus to Rufus.

And Rufus was squirming in his wheelchair.

The Tainted were emotion and instinct, and according to the elves, fed off of the negative emotions of humans. They liked to cause havoc and chaos. Knowing that made me all kinds of nervous all of the sudden.

"Human," Wyatt said, and I knew it was the Tainted taking control this time. "You reek of shame when presented with my host's form. Why?"

I looked at Kismet, whose eyes went wide with understanding. Astrid, bless her, was oblivious to the undercurrent and said, "Who cares? You three have a mission to prepare for. You can talk about your feelings later."

"Good plan," I said. "Whatever Wyatt and Rufus have to work out, it's between them, not the entire group of us. Shelve it."

Wyatt stared Rufus down for several long seconds, before visibly standing down.

Another disaster averted. If Rufus admitted his secret while Wyatt was still holding the Tainted, Rufus would be dead in seconds. Wyatt wouldn't be able to stop himself because of the Tainted's influence, and he'd regret it for the rest of his life.

"Excellent," Astrid said. "Let's get weapons."

Strapping on extra knives and a few guns had never felt so much like preparation for a kamikaze attack. As if a part of me had accepted the fact that we might not come back from First Break. No one could predict how the Fey would react to our invasion. Evacuation? All out war? Trolls shaking the entire little underground community apart and leaving us to our deaths?

The Tainted were all given their choice of sharp objects. Wyatt and Marcus both chose machetes, and Phineas requested his own ancient Coni blade.

Aurora, Astrid and Kismet followed us to the Sanctuary door. Isleen hadn't locked it from our entry this morning. No one said goodbye or good luck. I don't think anyone knew what to say. All we had left was hope and stubbornness.

And luck.

Verbalized or not, we really, really needed luck on our side this time.

Power from the Break rippled through me. All three of the men with me seemed to calm a bit under its spell.

Magic called to all of us. I placed them in a circle, Wyatt on my right and Marcus on my left. Wyatt and I described every detail we could remember about First Break so that everyone could imagine it in their heads while we teleported.

"Hold hands, boys," I said.

Their skin was hotter than I expected, and a soft bolt of energy went from Wyatt to me as our taps merged. Nerves wormed through my stomach. I closed my eyes and drew on my emotional tap. Power flooded through me from the Break and from Wyatt, buzzing across my skin and setting it on fire. I collected everything I could, held it close, and then we broke apart.

We fell into the Break.

So much power. So much more than at any other time in my life—even during that thunderstorm. We whipped about, caught in its current, and I focused hard on First Break. On that waterfall and the pool of water below. To the sandy spot nearby. Our destination.

The farther we went, moving through the earth itself, the less power I could hold onto. My grip became a fragile thing as my mortal body protested the sheer amount of magic I was channeling. I wasn't built for this. I was losing it….

Until a blast of power from all three Tainted sent us barreling toward the end. I felt the sand beneath my feet, and I let go. Wyatt eased my collapse, and I knew by the rush of flowing water and the floral scents invading my nose that we'd made it.

Blood flowed down my upper lip, my body felt like jelly, and my head hurt like hell, but I was awake and aware.

First Break looked the same. Thousands of exotic flowers growing in the rocky walls that stretched up for hundreds of feet into darkness. The waterfall that ended in a glassy black pool that didn't ripple, despite the constant motion. The small city that had been dug out of the rock itself, with doors and windows and walkways zigzagging up at least twelve stories. Basketball-sized spheres glowing with orange light. Gold and silver and gems decorating everything.

Beautiful.

And deadly.

"That sure beat being vomited up by a troll," Wyatt said.

I almost laughed. "Sure did."

Our voices echoed in the seemingly empty cavern. But we weren't alone. Someone had left the lights on.

The ground beneath us rumbled, as if a train was speeding by in close proximity.

Wyatt helped me stand, and all three men stood in a kind of triangle with Phineas at the point, and me protected behind them. Not that I needed them to protect me, but I was still a little shaky after transport so the support was nice.

"Amalie," Phineas said, his deep voice bouncing off the rock walls. "You have much to answer for, Sprite Queen."

"Have I now?" her disembodied voice replied. It floated from all directions, making pinpointing her location impossible. "You dare soil my home with your presence?"

"You've brought this upon yourself. At least have the courage to face us."

She appeared from behind a door on the third level—not the door I remembered going into during our first visit to this place. Barely four feet tall, Amalie's true form had sky blue skin, ruby red lips, and flaming red hair spiraled and decorated with crystals. Other crystals decorated her skin all over her sexless body. She carried no weapons that I could see.

"I had thought to spare your life for your persistence and ingenuity, Evangeline," Amalie said. "You bringing these creatures here has sealed your death."

Like I haven't heard that one before.

Keeping that thought to myself rose my self-preservation skill level to expert.

"You seem nervous, Sprite," Marcus said. "What have you to say when faced with those you have condemned?"

"You condemned yourself when you thought you were superior to us. When you put your desires above everyone else and made the human race your playthings. Your subjugates."

"Didn't you do the same thing with the vampire race?" I asked. "They were your slaves and you made them dependant on the blood of humans."

Amalie's slow blink was her only actual sign of surprise. "Your elf allies have been telling stories, I see."

"All kinds of stories. And they don't exactly paint the Fey as the beacon of hope for humanity. The elves wanted to leave so humans could take their rightful place as rulers over this planet, and the rest of you got feisty. You banished the Tainted and you eradicated most of the elves, and now they all want a little payback. You've manipulated the Triads for the last ten years, you have caused numerous unnecessary deaths, and now *we* want a little payback, too."

Amalie made a sound like a whistle, only more musical. A buzzing cloud poured out of the doorways and windows on two of the top levels. It sparkled as it descended, and I recognized the cluster of faeries from before. Higher above them was another cloud, this made of little lights the size of fireflies—and thanks to a little lesson from Brevin, I also knew the pixies way up there had razor sharp teeth and painful bites.

Nothing like being eaten to death my massive mosquitoes.

From the bottom two levels came dozens of creatures I couldn't name, a mixed bag like before. Some proportionate like Amalie, others not so much. Many with jewels, all with oddly colored skin. They formed ranks in front of Amalie, protecting her from us with their own bodies. No physical weapons, but they lived at the source of all magic, so I wasn't underestimating anybody.

"We have no quarrel with you," Phineas said to the group at large. "We have quarrel with the sprite you protect. Only one life has to be taken this day."

"I agree," Amalie said. "Kill the human Evangeline Stone, and you three may remain in this world to live as you like. I will even see that your missing kin is freed and returned to you."

Uh oh.

The fact that neither of my three allies spoke up immediately told me how strongly the Tainted were in control. Being this close to the source of all magic, to the portal back to their original world, had to be messing with the control that Wyatt, Phineas and Marcus had over their demons.

"We have already given our word to another," Wyatt said. "We must see that bargain through before a new one can be made."

I would never, in this world or the next, tell Wyatt how relieved I was to hear him say that.

Amalie's eyes twitched. Bitch wasn't used to being told no. Maybe we'd luck out and she was bluffing. I mean, the magic critters in front of us didn't look like they'd put up much of a fight, no matter how ferociously the dwarves had attacked.

"Wait," Phineas said.

My heart flipped. Phin was smart and super-observant. He also wasn't a traitor, demon or not.

Please have a plan.

He took three steps forward, away from our cluster, and at the front line of Amalie's guardians. They didn't move, and they didn't attack.

"Your elder has spoken for you, Elash," Amalie said. "What more is there to say?"

Okay, the fact that Amalie knew the Tainted by name was uber-creepy.

"Perhaps he speaks for Elash, but he does not speak for my host," Phineas replied. "He does not speak for the Coni whose race was destroyed by human hands."

"You call this human your ally and friend, Coni. Why would you turn against her at this late hour?"

"To end the bloodshed. She is one woman out of millions. Her life is an acceptable trade if it restores order to our world."

Wyatt growled deep in his throat, the threat waking up his inner Lupa. I grabbed his wrist and squeezed, silently begging him to stay still and trust Phineas. Phineas wouldn't give me up. He wouldn't.

Amalie studied him a moment. "And what would you trade her life for? What do you ask of me in return?"

"What the elves asked for so many millennia ago—a complete withdrawal from the world of humankind. Allow them to evolve without interference. Without whispering in the ears of politicians and world leaders. Without manipulating them into hunting other living creatures because you desire it."

"You ask much for the life of one human."

"One human who has, for months, defied your expectations and ruined your carefully laid plans at every turn. A thorn in your side who has brought three Tainted, your greatest enemy, into the heart of your home. You wish her head and you lack the ability to do it yourself." Phineas glanced around the buzzing cavern. "And my instincts tell me your underlings lack that ability, as well."

"You assume much, Coni."

"And yet you deny nothing. Our presence here unnerves you, Sprite Queen. We can slaughter you and your people in minutes, and you cannot stop us."

I worked hard to stop a smile. Phineas was totally calling her bluff.

For the first time ever, Amalie was nervous and uncertain. Sprites didn't improvise well or quickly. They planned long because they lived long. She didn't expect us to show up in First Break, and now we held all the cards.

"I think it's a fair bargain," Marcus said. "The human female for your withdrawal from our lives."

Wyatt growled again and took a long step backward, which made me retreat, too. Part of him was probably acting, but the rest of him was instinctively reacting to a threat against his mate. "I won't let you kill her," he said. "She's mine."

"Forget the human, father. We can remain here, in this world."

"That is not the bargain we made. We must honor what we told the elves."

"No. No, Isash and I agree on this," Phineas said. "She dies." He stepped forward again, and this time the line of fair folk parted so they didn't get stepped on. His massive form worked its way through them to stand an arm's reach from Amalie.

She stared up at him, outwardly un-intimidated. Her brain had to be whirring, though, wondering what to do next.

"Do we have a bargain, you and I?" Phineas asked. "Your fair folk leave us to our own futures, without interference, and she dies."

Amalie did that slow-blink thing. "Agreed. Myself and my people will abide by this agreement."

"Excellent."

Phineas grabbed Amalie by the throat with his left hand and rose into the sky in a rush of air from his massive wings. The ancient blade flashed in his right hand an instant before he buried it in her skull. Gold blood dripped like glitter onto the other fair folk, who gaped at the move none of them saw coming.

He dropped the body into their midst. "Amalie's mistake," he said, "was in not clarifying which 'she' was to die. Blood has been spilled. You will honor the agreement, or you will be hunted."

The buzzing cloud of pixies and faeries disappeared, as did the fey on the ground. All retreated to the stone city, until only Amalie's corpse remained in the sandy courtyard. I stared at her, unable to believe she was truly dead. That maybe so much of the turmoil from the last ten years was finally coming to an end.

Yeah, right, tell that to the city full of people reporting Halfie and goblin attacks all over the place.

We had cleaning up to do, but this chapter was finally fucking over.

Go team.

"Nice bluff there, Phin," I said.

The glare I got in return did not instill me with confidence. "Do not thank me yet, human. We battled, your friend and I."

Oh great, Edash was winning. "Well, I think we all made out pretty okay. You kept your bargain with Brevin, and we'll keep ours with you. You get your kin back."

"And then we go."

"As agreed."

The three Tainted shared a look I didn't like, but no one contradicted me.

"What now?" Wyatt asked.

"Now we go home," I said. "All of us."

CHAPTER SIXTEEN

After dispatching Amalie, I spent the next little while accidentally unconscious. Apparently teleporting across the city and through solid earth twice in an hour took a pretty terrible toll on one's body, and I passed out the instant we reappeared in the Sanctuary. I was impressed I hadn't lost power halfway and teleported us into the middle of Mercy's Lot, so a power nap was a win in my book.

I woke up on a cot in one of the infirmary's curtained exam rooms. The IV surprised me but I was probably dehydrated. My bladder confirmed that the bag was almost empty, so I tugged the needle out of my arm.

"Hello?" I called out as I sat up. My body still ached a bit in the joints, but I didn't fall over or get dizzy.

Footsteps shuffled toward my curtain. Kismet pulled it back, her eyes red and puffy, and my heart shot into my throat.

"Is it Milo?" I asked.

"It's a lot of things," she replied. "Milo's still fighting the virus. He's hanging on."

"How about our guys? Shit, how long have I been out?"

"Two hours."

"Damn." Damn. "Did they sent the Tainted back?"

She nodded. "According to Brevin, removing the Tainted went as he expected. All four were sent back across the Break."

Thank Christ. "And what about Wyatt? Phin? Marcus? How are they?"

"They're in rooms receiving medical attention."

I lurched to my feet, pleased I managed to stay on them and not face-plant. "What does that mean? How are they? Are they injured?"

"Yes, they are. Their transformations were both magical and physical. Severe muscle strains, bruising, some stress fractures. They are all massively dehydrated and suffering from major exhaustion."

"It's all recoverable stuff, though, right?"

"According to Dr. Vansis, yes. Marcus and Phineas have both been briefly conscious."

My heart slammed into my ribs. "But Wyatt hasn't?"

"No." Kismet swallowed hard. "He's half-human still. The effects were far worse for him."

Bladder forgotten, I pushed past her, beyond the curtained area, and stalked down the hallway to the patient rooms. Milo was in the first one, Marcus and Phineas the second. The two Therians were both unconscious and looked like they'd been through a war—all kinds of bruising mottled their exposed skin, all kinds of bandages. Wires and IV lines hooked up in several places.

But aside from the external damage, they looked like themselves again and that was everything.

I hesitated at the next door, reluctant to see Wyatt in another hospital bed. The last time had been during his fight against the Lupa virus—a fight that left him forever changed. I still loved the man he'd become, and I would continue to love whoever I found on the other side of that door.

Then Kismet was there, and she opened the door for me. I took a step inside and my heart nearly stopped.

Wyatt had never looked so still or vulnerable or…delicate, than in that moment. His skin was one large bruise, a palette of blues and purples and greens, like he'd been beaten to within an inch of his life. His eyes were swollen shut. Both of his hands were in splits, all fingers bandaged. His IV stand included a bag of blood slowly dripping into his left arm. Even the rise and fall of his chest barely registered.

I eased onto the edge of the bed and brushed gentle fingertips across his lips, the only spot on his body that seemed okay to touch. "I'm here, Wyatt. I'm here, and I love you so much. So much."

I didn't expect a reaction, but the lack thereof still hurt a little.

"We did it, babe. We won. Amalie is dead and this thing she began back in April is finally fucking over. We get to have our happy ending, you and me." Tears stung my eyes, and I swallowed hard against a rising tide of grief. "We get our beach with fruity drinks and no more hunting. No more fighting."

Nothing.

"How are the Lupa pups holding up?" I asked after a few minutes of silence.

"They're terrified of everyone, especially other Therians," Kismet replied, "so we're keeping them isolated. We've brought them food and water, but they won't touch it."

"I'll go see them soon. Maybe it'll help calm them down." They'd need to hear from someone they trusted that Wyatt was still alive. "What's happening in the city?"

"We pulled all of the Coni out because police and news helicopters were crowding the skies. A few injuries but no fatalities."

"Good. Squads?"

"A dozen or so still on the ground, mostly cleaning up messes and responding to the occasional report, but overall activity is down to almost nothing. It's as if the moment Amalie died, her minions stopped attacking."

"Kind of like the goblins when Nessa died. Guess those queen bitches weren't so different after all."

"Guess not."

"How did we do with fatalities?"

"None, thank God. A few serious injuries, and Nevada somehow managed to get arrested for carrying an illegal firearm. Astrid is still strategizing how to get him out of that mess."

I couldn't help it. The image of Seth Nevada, a Handler from the original Triads, being arrested by the police made me laugh. That first peel of laughter turned into a giggle fit that had me on the floor, eyes streaming tears, stomach aching from the force of it. At some point, the laughing turned to actual tears.

Kismet sat next to me and squeezed my arm while I worked it through. The release left me more exhausted than ever, but goddamn, I'd needed that. Needed to get out all of the insanity and fear from the last twenty-four hours. It wouldn't totally go away until all four men in hospital beds were up and back to their old selves, but it was a good start.

"Feel better?" she asked.

"Yeah." I stared up at the ceiling, too tired to sit back up until absolutely necessary. "Thank you."

"It's what friends are for."

"You know, growing up I rarely had anyone in my corner. No real friends. Not until Jesse and Ash took me under their wings and made me part of their team. After they died I honestly never thought I'd have real friends again. Friends I'd die to protect." I sat up on a rush of gratitude and respect. "Thank you for being my friend, Gina Kismet."

Kismet grinned. "Well, considering I did try to blow you up surrounded by vats of gremlin piss, I'm pretty honored to be your friend now, Evy. You were a mouthy pain in the ass as a Hunter, but you've become a strong leader. If you and Wyatt really do leave, this organization is going to miss you. So will I."

I needed to shift gears before this got too touchy-feely. "Hey, we'll only be a plane ticket away. Plus maybe a puddle-jump to a tiny island."

"Sounds good to me."

I kissed Wyatt lightly on the mouth before leaving the infirmary. A Coni female stood at attention outside of the door to our jail area, which had several reinforced interrogation cells. They'd finally been rebuilt after being blown up a few weeks ago. She let me go inside with no fuss. The boys were huddled in the middle of a silver-treated room, staying away from the walls and clinging to each other.

My heart ached for them, so young and terrified. Even if they looked up, they wouldn't see me because of the two-way mirror. I un-snapped the deadbolts on my side and opened it. All three of them flinched in unison.

"It's me," I said.

Three heads snapped up, and their fear shifted into genuine smiles.

"You're back," Peter said.

"I said I'd come back for you. It's just been a long morning." I nudged at the tray with sandwiches and bottled water. "Please eat. I promise you that it isn't poisoned. No one would do that." No one moved, so I picked up a ham and cheese on white and took a big bite. My own hunger kicked it and I ate half the sandwich before putting it back.

The boys exchanged quick looks, then dove for the food.

"Wyatt's alive, too," I said while they ate. "He's very hurt and he has a lot of recovering to do, but he's alive."

"And your friend?" Mark asked, so tentative it made me want to cry. "The man I bit? How is he?"

"Fighting. Fighting hard."

"Will I be executed for biting him?"

"Over my dead body. You were manipulated into an action because you thought John's life was at risk. I won't let the Assembly kill you for that, even if I have to smuggle you out of the country."

"I don't understand why you continue to risk so much for us," Peter said.

"You're part of Wyatt, and Wyatt is a part of me. Hence, we're part of each other, so I get to protect you from politicians and big, bad were-cats who might want revenge."

"Revenge?"

"Milo? My friend who was bitten? He has a Felia boyfriend who was really pissed off when he found out what happened. He's kind of unconscious right now, so we've got some time to figure out how to keep him from flipping his shit. Trust me, okay?"

"We do."

"Good. I'll be back in a while. I've got something else to take care of."

John surprised me by standing up and hugging me. A very quick one, but it meant the world to me for him to do that. I locked them back in, then made my way toward the dorms.

Not that a shower and change of clothes was on the agenda. One more errand before I could see to myself. The door no longer had a guard, which didn't surprise me, and the keys were on the floor nearby. I unlocked it and let myself in.

Stephen and Lori Frost were on opposite sides of the room, both of them silent. Stephen put down a newspaper, and Lori dropped a novel someone must have given her to pass the time. I stepped away from the open door. "Time to leave."

They exchanged a look.

Stephen huffed. "Please tell me you're ready to be reasonable and see a therapist."

I cackled longer than necessary because, yeah, not all out of my system yet. "Pal, if I'm going to see a therapist for any reason, it's going to be for PTSD, not because I'm delusional about my identity. Chalice is dead. I'm Evangeline Stone. I'm not your daughter."

"Why are you releasing us now?" Lori asked in a timid voice.

"Because me teleporting? The big cats you saw shifting? There's no sense in hiding it. Through circumstances of someone else's making, the city is pretty well aware that there are a lot of creatures out there going bump in the night. You won't be telling a tale any taller than anyone else on the street."

"Is that what all that noise was?"

"Yup. That was the sound of the shit hitting the paranormal fan. It's not fair to keep you here anymore. You two have a daughter to grieve, and a new reality to accept. I'll have someone drive you into the city."

Lori stood and took a tentative step toward me. "You can't do it yourself, Chal-Evangeline?"

At least one of them was starting to accept reality. "No, I have business here. Take care of yourselves, okay?"

"I just…please?"

"What?"

She came a little closer, until I could see the grief etched all over her face. A face so much like mine. "I think I accept what you're saying, honey, but...may I have one last hug? You still look so much like her."

What kind of cold, dead heart says no to a question like that?

I let Lori hug me for a long time, and she cried a little bit. I patted her back and allowed her to grieve her daughter. Stephen kept his distance, a skeptic until the end. Their marriage might not survive this, and that couldn't be helped. My life was with Wyatt, not with them.

We practically tripped over Paul in the corridor, and he agreed to drive them—blindfolded, of course—to their hotel. I walked with them to the parking area, then hugged Paul for the favor, because apparently I was in a hugging mood today. Astrid might rip me a new one for releasing them without using the memory potion, but I didn't care. Their daughter was dead.

It was time for the Frosts to move on.

It was also beyond time for me to take a fucking shower.

Squeaky clean and finally in new clothes, I swung by the cafeteria for a sandwich and water, then ate on my walk back to the infirmary. As our people trickled back in, more and more faces crowded the corridor and mingled in groups. I got a few cheers and congratulations for taking down Amalie that I politely acknowledged as I passed.

Phineas got all the credit on that one, not me. I was simply the mode of transportation.

The sandwich went down fast, and I'd chugged half the water bottle by the time I got to the infirmary. Kismet surprised me by loitering in the hall outside of Milo's room. The door was shut.

"Dr. Vansis doing an exam?" I asked.

"No." Her green eyes were wide and, surprisingly, hopeful. "The elves asked to see him in private. Actually, they kind of insisted."

"Why? They said they couldn't do anything for Wyatt."

"I don't know, Evy, but if there's a chance they can help Milo I'm going to let them. I still haven't accepted that Tybalt's gone. I can't lose him too."

"I know. Anyone else awake?"

"Phin woke up for a few minutes. Said a few words, but he's in so much pain that Dr. Vansis knocked him out again. He'll sleep for a few hours yet. Marcus is stirring but he's likely in as much pain as Phin."

Wyatt was probably in twice as much pain—or he would be when he finally came back to me.

We took turns pacing the hallway, occasionally popping our heads in to check on our guys. Dr. Vansis slipped past us twice to check on other patients in other rooms without a remark. Close to an hour passed before the door to Milo's room creaked open.

Sorvin exited first, followed by the elf whose name I never caught. Brevin came out last and he approached us with what probably passed for a smile in his world. "Your friend will be all right," he said.

"He will?" Kismet squeaked.

"How?" I asked. "You couldn't fix Wyatt's infection."

"Wyatt's physical form had already been transformed by the Lupa virus. We cannot reverse what nature has already created. In your friend Milo's cause, the infection had not yet won. His immune system was fighting against it, so no permanent damage had been done. My brothers and I were able to isolate and collect the virus, and then contain it within his body. He has a mark now, in the center of his chest."

I stared, trying to wrap my brain around that. "You turned the Lupa virus into a magical tattoo?"

Brevin nodded. "You are very colorful with your words, Evangeline. You amuse me."

"Happy to help."

"As are my brothers and I. We did what we set out to do, and your peoples were instrumental in breaking the Fey's hold over this world. My kin's magic will die with us soon. We may as well use it to help for whatever time we have left."

"Thank you so much," Kismet said as she dashed past him.

"Yeah, me too." I followed her into Milo's room, my heart in my throat, not daring to hope.

Milo was sitting up in bed, his color normal, staring beneath the front of his hospital gown. He dropped it when Kismet threw herself at him for a hug. I ignored her tears, and then I ignored my own tears when I joined them for a three-way, smushing Milo between us.

"I know a big kitty cat who's going to be so happy to see you," I said, then kissed his cheek. "Boring old brown eyes and all."

"I'll take brown," Milo replied. "I was so fucking scared of this thing. Not even of dying from it but of having to live with it like Wyatt does. He snarls at Marcus so much. I didn't...I mean...."

"We know what you mean." Being half-Lupa could have blown apart the delicate thing that he and Marcus were trying to create.

Happiness and love.

We let him sit up, and it was the best sight in the world. He flexed his bandaged shoulder, then peeked beneath. "Hey, that's fixed too."

So was the gash on his forearm, apparently. And the lingering pain from his torture session.

"If Brevin is your type, I'd say he deserves a big wet one for all this," I said.

Milo laughed. "I feel better than I have in ages, to be honest. And look." He pulled down the hospital gown, showing off what looked like a cat's paw inked in brown.

The virus.

"Not how I'd have suggested going about getting your first tattoo, but it works." I wiggled my eyebrows. "Marcus is going to love it."

"Can I go see him? Please? I feel fine, I swear."

"Of course."

He scrambled out of the room faster than either me or Kismet, and he was already by Marcus's bed, gently holding one bandaged hand in his, by the time we got there.

"Hey, big guy," he said. "I defied the odds and got better, so it's your turn. We got this far. Time for us to see what's next, yeah?"

I tugged on Kismet's hand, and we left. Milo was fine, and he deserved some time alone with his guy. Well, as alone as they were with someone sleeping in the next bed. I went to sit with Wyatt for a while. There was absolutely nothing else on earth that I needed to be doing besides that.

And it felt wonderful.

CHAPTER SEVENTEEN

Phineas was out of his hospital bed and hobbling around the Watchtower corridors less than twenty-four hours after expelling the Tainted, and completely against doctor's orders. The stubborn ass didn't surprise me. He wanted in on everything going on, including the decision of six of the Coni warriors—Pike included—to stay in the city.

Aurora was returning to Greece by the end of the week to be with Ava, and when Ava was of age, she would be allowed to decide where she lived. But for Ava's mother, this city was no longer home.

It no longer felt much like my home anymore, but I kept that to myself.

Marcus sprung himself from the infirmary about eight hours after Phineas, and I think he only hung around a little longer because he secretly loved the way Milo pampered him—and only left his side for food and personal hygiene reasons.

Not that I could fault Milo his dedication. I did the same thing with Wyatt, by his side as often as possible, reading books and just talking to him. Waiting for him to finally wake up and show me his beautiful silver-flecked black eyes.

On the second day, I left the Watchtower to appear before the Assembly of Clan Elders.

The Voice of the Assembly, a Cania man named Olso, picked me up at noon and drove us east, into a low-rent residential area. Crumbling row homes, weedy front lawns, cars on cinderblocks. He pulled into a parking lot that serviced several discount stores. Everything about this moment was familiar. Months ago, Wyatt and Michael Jenner had accompanied me here to speak to the Assembly for the first time.

Funny how they still met in the exact same location.

I followed Oslo into a flooring emporium. The sharp smell of new carpet and the waxy smell of tiles and wax tickled my nose. Like the first time, we navigated our way through the cavernous space, past rolls of linoleum and shelves of remnants, to the very back. Through a door marked Employees Only. Past a break room that still reeked of cigarette smoke and grease.

To a big gray door marked Private.

The entire way, I'd tried to put out of my mind the reason for this audience. Now that I was faced with it, my pulse raced and my palms went clammy.

I was here to argue for three lives.

Oslo opened the door and held it so I could enter ahead of him. As before, a bright light shined down at me, making it difficult to see the men and women of the

Assembly. Many I already knew, but not all of them. And I couldn't resent them their privacy.

The door shut with a hard clink.

"Evangeline Stone." Elder Rojay. "This is twice you have come before the Assembly of Clan Elders. A record for a human, as only three others have ever come but once."

"I am honored that you have given up your time to hear me today," I said.

"You know why you are here."

"Yes."

"The three Lupa you protect were given leniency by this Assembly under the express promise that they infect no more human beings," a familiar voice said. Deep Throat. He was the Kitsune Elder. "One of them broke that promise two days ago."

"I know." I looked in the general direction of his voice. "I'm here to take responsibility for the actions of the three Lupa under my protection."

"They are under the protection of the half-breed Wyatt Truman."

Anger fluttered under my breast bone. "Wyatt Truman is currently recovering from life-threatening wounds sustained in the course of stopping the sprite Amalie from unleashing chaos upon this world. And as Wyatt's chosen mate, I am able to speak for him."

A soft murmur went through the room.

"You continue to surprise me, Ms. Stone," Deep Throat said. "Never before has a human come to this Assembly to ask us to spare the lives of Therians."

"I've surprised a lot of people recently, Elder, including myself." I looked around the room at faces I couldn't see. "A month ago, I never would have imagined myself the protector of three—if you'll pardon the expression—werewolf teenagers. But they are not the monsters of your history. They have names. John, Mark and Peter.

"Yes, they have made mistakes. Yes, their slain brothers are responsible for many deaths. But these boys were given to a madman to raise. They were sheltered from the world and from real love. They were programmed to do Walter Thackery's bidding without question. All they want is a chance to have a real life."

"They were given that chance once," Elder Rojay said. "And one of them chose to bite a human. Your friend, if I'm not mistaken."

"Yes, Mark bit my friend. Yes, my friend Milo got sick, but he did not transform as Wyatt did. An elf ally was able to isolate and contain the Lupa virus. Milo does not wish to see the Lupa boys punished. He's already submitted a video statement saying so."

"This is not a human court of law." A familiar female voice this time. "Your friend cannot simply refuse to press charges. The safety of other innocent lives is our greatest concern."

"The safety of innocent lives has been my greatest concern for the last four-plus years of my life. And the last few months of my afterlife." The tiny attempt at humor fell flat, so I went on. "These three boys' greatest strength is their love for each other. And it's also their greatest weakness. Amalie exploited that weakness two days ago. She convinced Peter and Mark that John's life was in imminent danger. She deceived them into believing a false outcome, and they reacted out of fear. They reacted out of instinct. They reacted to save their brother. That is an instinct that is alive in every person in this room, be it Therian or human. Am I wrong?"

Utter silence was my answer.

"We all act impulsively when those we love are threatened," I said. "So I am asking for your mercy. Spare their lives, and I will ensure they are no longer a threat to anyone in this city."

"And how will you do that?" Elder Dane asked, speaking up for the first time.

"By leaving the city with them."

Another soft murmur rose. Guess I surprised them with that one.

"You're leaving the city?" Elder Dane said. "For how long?"

"Forever, if it's up to me. Wyatt and I had already discussed it. We've both shed enough blood for this city and its people. We want to take the boys and go. Far away from here."

"You have been a great asset to the Watchtower, Ms. Stone. Your contributions will be missed."

"Everyone retires at some point, Elder. I may be leaving with a lot of nightmares instead of a 401k, but that's fine. This is what I want, and quite frankly? I think it's the least I deserve."

Someone spoke in that weird secret language of theirs.

"Have you anything else to say to the Assembly?" Deep Throat asked.

"I've said what I came here to say." And for once, I found my inner snark failing me. I truly respected the men and women in this room. They made difficult decisions in order to protect the anonymity of their Clans. To help them successfully live their lives among humans and vampires year after year, generation after generation. "Thank you for hearing me out. It's been an honor working with the Assembly these last few months."

"Good journey to you, Evangeline Stone," Elder Rojay said.

"And to you all."

"We will inform you of our decision by tomorrow evening."

Oslo followed me out of the room. I paused long enough to let my vision adjust to the dim light of the hallway.

"That went well, I guess," I said.

"You are a passionate speaker." Olso led the way back toward the showroom. "It works well in your favor that you plan to leave the city with the Lupa. As long as that was true."

"Trust me, it's true. I'm ready for a permanent vacation."

I spent the rest of the day alternating my time between Wyatt's room and our apartment—to which the boys had been allowed to return. The holding cell hadn't been good for their nerves or their overall mental state. I wasn't a fan of the exterior deadbolt on our door, but hey, house arrest beat jail.

I also didn't go anywhere near Ops. Whatever was going on, I didn't care. We had people doing repair work on damage sustained by the earthquake. We had people in the field. No emergency klaxons were blaring. Nothing serious had happened in two days, which was kind of a record, and I didn't want to jinx anything by getting involved.

Around nine o'clock that night, after I closed and put down the book I'd been reading to Wyatt, I looked up and into the silver-flecked black eyes I knew and loved so much. Time stopped for a moment, until he blinked and broke the spell.

"Hey," I said. My throat tightened and nothing else came out.

He blinked again, his dry lips quirking into a half-smile. I moved from my chair to perch on the bed next to him. Held one of his bandaged hands in mine.

I swallowed hard against so much rising emotion and finally found words. "We did it. We won."

His gaze moved all over, taking in my body.

"I'm fine," I said. "No additional damage for once."

He grunted.

"Marcus and Phineas are doing well. Both still healing from the ordeal, but they're alive and so are you. And so are the pups. I went to the Assembly and asked for leniency. We'll know their decision by tomorrow night."

His eyebrows rose.

"Don't look so surprised, Truman. I care about those boys, too. Mark reacted out of love for his brother. I won't let him be punished for that."

He licked his lips, and I could have slapped myself. I grabbed the glass of soda I'd brought in with me and dug out a piece of ice. I smoothed it over his lips, allowing him to suck in some of its moisture, not caring that my fingertips were going numb.

"Thanks," he said, his voice raspy and worn. But it was Wyatt's voice, no longer dark and threatening from the Tainted's control. My Wyatt.

"I'd ask how you feel, but you're obviously in pain. Do you need anything? Should I call Dr. Vansis?"

"Just need you." He tried squeezing my hands. "Love you so much."

"Me too. I knew you'd come back to me."

"I didn't know. Tainted was so strong, Evy."

"But you were stronger."

His eyes flashed with so many different emotions I couldn't count them all. "Can still feel him. His hate and rage. Scares me."

"It's okay." I pressed a kiss to his forehead. "We'll get through it. Together. Know why?"

"Because you're stuck with me?"

I laughed. "Because we got our happy ending. It's you and me and three werewolf puppies against the world."

He rasped a sound that might have been a chuckle. "Wouldn't want it any other way."

"Good."

This time I kissed his lips, a gentle press that was also a promise. We were in this together, no matter what.

Aurora and most of the other Coni left at midnight. We hugged for a long time on the Watchtower roof.

"Come visit us if you can," she said. "Ava would love to see you."

"I'd love to see her." Ava was probably the size of a toddler by now. I pulled back, my eyes stinging. "We came a long way from stashing you and Joseph in Chalice's apartment."

"We have. You did yourself proud in protecting us, Evangeline. Don't ever doubt that."

"You did yourself proud, too, Aurora. You fought for your people. You did *me* proud."

She grinned. "Thank you. I'll see you again."

"Yes, you will."

I stood there with Astrid and Phineas as the clutch of Coni warriors rose into the sky on a rush of wind and the gentle beating of their massive wings. So beautiful against inky blue and a faint scattering of visible stars. We stood there until they disappeared, and I knew a little bit of Phineas's heart went with them. He still hadn't decided on his next step—go to Greece to be with his kin, or stay here and continue to help the Watchtower.

I had a funny feeling the reason for his indecision had red hair and a killer left hook.

Astrid descended the ladder first, leaving me and Phin alone.

"She was right, you know," he said after a few minutes of companionable silence.

I didn't have to clarify that he meant Aurora. "Right about what?"

"You did yourself proud. You did the Coni and Stri people proud."

"Yeah, well, you did trick me into helping you."

He laughed, a musical sound that I'd almost never heard again. "That I did. And yet we still became friends."

"Very good friends." I wrapped a loose around his waist without leaning in too hard. He was still healing and in moderate amounts of pain—even if he'd never admit it. "I'm going to miss you."

"And I'll miss you. But we'll see each other again in the future. In some place or another."

"Definitely. You have a standing invitation to visit wherever it is Wyatt and I end up settling."

"Thank you."

"As long as you bring Gina with you."

He sighed. "You are relentless."

"Yes I am. Can't help it. After all of the shit we've survived, we all deserve happiness and someone to share it with."

"Yes, we do. And whatever Gina and I are, or are not, to each other, that is for us to define."

I laughed out loud. "Is that your way of telling me to mind my own business?"

"In so many words."

Never change, Phineas el Chimal. Never change.

Milo was waiting for us at the bottom of the ladder, looking happier and healthier than he had in weeks. Whatever the elves did to isolate the Lupa virus had also healed everything that had ailed him. "You aren't answering your phone."

"I turned it off," I replied. "What's up?"

"I was hoping you'd be up for a sparring match. I haven't worked out in forever."

Hearing those words made my heart leap for joy. "Definitely. It's been a while since I kicked your ass on the mat."

"Bring it, Stone."

"Gladly. You gonna have your kitty cat there to protect you?"

Milo growled. I knuckled his shoulder, then led the way down the service corridor.

This was going to be fun.

LATER

Numerous peals of joyous laughter rouse me from a dreamless nap. I blink the scene into focus behind the shade of my sunglasses. And the sight makes me smile.

Mark, John and Peter are splashing in the surf caused by low tide, taking turns seeing who can create the largest wave by stomping their feet in the swirling water. All three are soaked, their pinking skin glistening from their romp in the sea. Until yesterday, they'd never been out of the state, much less seen the ocean. Now they can't get enough. And our house is secluded enough that last night all three went for a midnight swim in their true forms.

I don't know how Wyatt found or afforded our little slice of tropical island, but here we are. A single-story beach house that is almost entirely windows. A quarter-mile of private beach with crystal-clear water. A golf cart for trips into the village for food and supplies. And the most beautiful weather I can ask for.

Paradise.

A hard-earned, well-deserved paradise.

Bonus points for having a very tiny Break on the other side of the island that hasn't seemed to attract much in the way of magical beings. Other than our quintet, of course.

I sent Milo photos this morning, and he's already threatening to visit. All of our friends know they're welcome at any time.

Except for Rufus. One day the fractured relationship between him and Wyatt may heal, but not anytime soon.

Two days before our scheduled departure, Rufus asked to speak with Wyatt in private. They were in the War Room, doors shut, for close to an hour. No one shouted. No furniture was thrown. Wyatt walked out in a oddly calm state, and Rufus wheeled out with a blackening right eye. Wyatt never told me exactly what was said, but in keeping that secret for so long, Rufus had violated ten years worth of built trust.

That sort of betrayal won't be fixed in a day. Maybe not even a year.

And forgiveness or not is up to Wyatt.

A gentle breeze stirs the air and brings the tang of salt with it. It tickles across my bare skin, which is already tanning under the midday sun. The first time I've ever worn a bathing suit, much less laid out in the sun for hours on end. I probably would have gone for a more modest one-piece, but Wyatt bought this royal blue bikini and I love it. Matches the blue swim trunks he bought for himself.

A tall, frosty glass full of pink liquid and topped with a paper umbrella appears in front of me. I take it with a smile, thirsty for my second Hurricane of the day. Wyatt isn't a master bartender, but he does a decent job with premade mixes. The fact that he tries makes them taste that much better.

He settles in the lounge chair next to mine with a matching pink drink, his sunglasses still perched on top of his head. His smile is unlike any smile I've seen on his face in the four and half years that I've known him. It's lazy and content and worry-free. The kind of smile I will never, ever take for granted.

I clink the rim of my glass against his, then take a sip. Fruity syrup and rum burst on my tongue, and I savor the warmth it spreads in my stomach.

John tackles Mark into the water, and Peter simply laughs at them.

So much laughter.

"I've never seen three teenage boys so happy in my life," Wyatt says.

"And just think. A year from now those teenagers are going to look as old us."

He chuckles, despite the oddly sobering thought. The boys are Therian, which means they will age rapidly. They have a lifespan of roughly twenty years total, three of which have been spent surviving, rather than experiencing. They won't want to stay on the island forever. And we won't keep them here if they choose to explore. Not once they're mature enough to do so.

It's also sobering for myself and Wyatt. No one knows if his half-Lupa state will increase how rapidly he ages. No one knows if my healing ability will slow down mine. All we know is that we won't take a single moment for granted. Not anymore.

I study his profile a moment. Black hair glimmering almost blue in the sunshine. Black eyes flecked with silver. Rugged features and a strong jaw that I know so well. The man I've been through hell and back with, and not once has he given up on me. Or on our happily ever after.

"Have I told you today how much I love you?" I ask him.

Wyatt turns his head, smiling. "Only once. This morning after we made love."

"In that case, I love you, Wyatt Truman."

"I love you too. For always."

For always.

My name is Evangeline Stone.

Six months ago I died and rose again. I vividly remember those first few moments, waking up in a morgue in someone else's body to the sounds of a woman screaming. I remember the names and faces of all the friends I've gained and lost since then. I honor them each day by living and loving as much as possible, and by never forgetting their loyalty and sacrifices.

The tension and bloodshed between the paranormal species of the world are far from over, but for now, my part in that story is over.

Today the sun rose on the first day of my third life—a life of peace and patience and love—and I can't wait to see what happens next.

THE END...KINDA

AUTHOR'S NOTE

From almost the very first page of *Three Days to Dead* I knew what the final scene of Evy and Wyatt's story would look like, and as I wrote it, the tears came. It's hard to say goodbye to characters that have lived in my head for more than seven years, but it's time. Evy has more than earned her happily ever after, and I hope you enjoyed her journey toward it.

Thank you for sticking with me all of these years and for supporting my books.

And if you're wondering about my "The End…Kinda", the Dreg City world is too vast for me to say it's over with. I'll come back and play in this sandbox again, believe me. Phineas, Kismet, Milo, Marcus, Astrid, and many other characters are still out there fighting the good fight. There will always be a need for the Watchtower Initiative.

As someone very famous once said, "I'll be back."

Made in United States
North Haven, CT
13 August 2023